"What's so romantic about going out with a complete stranger?"

Beth asked. "Everyone has been speculating about this romantic date I'm going to have with you, when all along I know it isn't the least bit romantic."

Kane threw back his head and laughed. "You really *are* innocent, aren't you?"

"What's that supposed to mean?"

"Most people are strangers until they get to know each other...which is usually through dating."

An embarrassed warmth crept up Beth's neck. "You know what I mean."

"Do I?"

He was being difficult, which should have annoyed her. Unfortunately, she was much too aware of Kane at the moment to be annoyed.

"I mean a date between two people who have never met and have no basis for attraction," she said.

"Ah." Kane leaned close until his arm touched hers, sending a startling warmth through her. "There's no basis for attraction, then. Between us?"

Dear Reader,

With summer nearly here, it's time to stock up on essentials such as sunblock, sandles and plenty of Silhouette Romance novels! Here's our checklist of page-turners to keep your days sizzling!

❑ *A Princess in Waiting* by Carol Grace (SR #1588)—In this ROYALLY WED: THE MISSING HEIR title, dashing Charles Rodin saves the day by marrying his brother's pregnant ex-wife!

❑ *Because of the Ring* by Stella Bagwell (SR #1589)—With this magical SOULMATES title, her grandmother's ring leads Claudia Westfield to the man of her dreams....

❑ *A Date with a Billionaire* by Julianna Morris (SR #1590)— Bethany Cox refused her prize—a date with the charitable Kane O'Rourke—but how can she get a gorgeous billionaire to take no for an answer? And does she really want to...?

❑ *The Marriage Clause* by Karen Rose Smith (SR #1591)— In this VIRGIN BRIDES installment, innocent Gina Foster agrees to a marriage of convenience with the wickedly handsome Clay McCormick, only to be swept into a world of passion.

❑ *The Man with the Money* by Arlene James (SR #1592)— A millionaire playboy in disguise romances a lovely foster mom. But will the truth destroy his chance at true love?

❑ *The 15 lb. Matchmaker* by Jill Limber (SR #1593)— Griff Price is the ultimate lone cowboy—until he's saddled with a baby and a jilted-bride-turned-nanny.

Be sure to come back next month for our list of great summer stories.

Happy reading!

Mary-Theresa Hussey
Senior Editor

A Date with a Billionaire

JULIANNA MORRIS

SILHOUETTE *Romance*

Published by Silhouette Books

America's Publisher of Contemporary Romance

To my nieces and nephews.

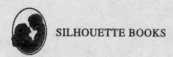 **SILHOUETTE BOOKS**

ISBN 0-373-19590-7

A DATE WITH A BILLIONAIRE

Copyright © 2002 by Martha Ann Ford

This edition published by arrangement with Harlequin Books S.A.

® and TM are trademarks of Harlequin Books S.A., used under license.
Trademarks indicated with ® are registered in the United States Patent
and Trademark Office, the Canadian Trade Marks Office and in other
countries.

Visit Silhouette at www.eHarlequin.com

Printed in U.S.A.

JULIANNA MORRIS

has an offbeat sense of humor, which frequently gets her into trouble. She is often accused of being curious about everything…her interests ranging from oceanography and photography to traveling, antiquing, walking on the beach and reading science fiction.

Julianna loves cats of all shapes and sizes, and last year she was adopted by a feline companion named Merlin. Like his namesake, Merlin is an alchemist—she says he can transform the house into a disaster area in nothing flat. And since he shares the premises with a writer, it's interesting to note that he's particularly fond of knocking books on the floor.

Julianna happily reports meeting Mr. Right. Together they are working on a new dream of building a shoreline home in the Great Lakes area.

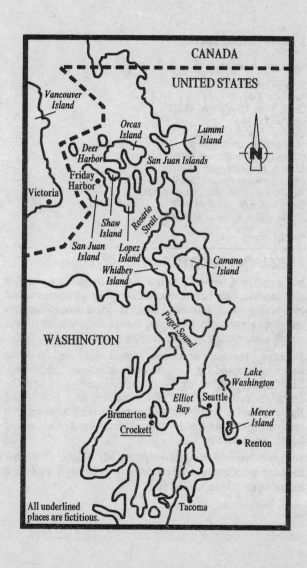

CANADA

UNITED STATES

Vancouver Island

Orcas Island

Lummi Island

Deer Harbor

San Juan Islands

Friday Harbor

Victoria

Shaw Island

Rosario Strait

San Juan Island

Lopez Island

Camano Island

Whidbey Island

WASHINGTON

Puget Sound

Lake Washington

Elliot Bay

Seattle

Mercer Island

Bremerton

Crockett

• Renton

All underlined places are fictitious.

Tacoma

Prologue

"**Y**ou've just won a date with a billionaire, Miss Cox," said the cheery voice on the phone.

Beth blinked and took a long look at the receiver, before putting it back to her ear. "Excuse me?"

"We're KLMS, the radio station for Your Country Music. And you've just won a weekend in romantic Victoria, British Columbia, with Kane O'Rourke, Seattle's most eligible bachelor!"

Stunned, Beth started to sit on a chair, missed it entirely and landed on the floor. "Ouch," she yelped.

"Are you all right, Miss Cox?"

"I just fell...on the floor."

A cheerful chuckle came over the line. "Hear that, folks? We should have told our prize winner to sit down first. Can you believe you just won, Miss Cox?"

"No. I...no."

"She's speechless, folks. Well, practically." The man chuckled again, apparently thinking he'd cracked a great joke.

"Uh, am I on the air?" Beth asked cautiously.

"Yes, ma'am. We just drew your name from the prize barrel."

Beth wasn't certain luck had anything to do with it, and she was even more certain she'd never entered the contest. She knew about it, of course. Half the town worked for Kane O'Rourke; he was one of Crockett, Washington's most prominent employers. And he was sinfully attractive. The contest was the only thing people had talked about since it was announced on the radio station.

"Do you have anything to say to our audience, Miss Cox? We're waiting to hear how you feel about your exciting prize."

"I think I'm..." She peered through her open door and saw her neighbor run up the walkway, waving a radio in the air.

"Oh, my God, you won," Carol shrieked as she darted inside the house. She snatched the receiver from Beth. "Hello? I'm Carol Hoit, one of Beth's best friends."

While Carol chattered away, Beth tried to sort things out in her head. Carol must have entered her in the contest. Two weeks before her neighbor had bemoaned the fact she couldn't qualify—being married—and had urged Beth to enter herself.

Lord...Beth rubbed her throbbing temples. She didn't want to go out with anyone. She'd lost her fiancé in an accident several years before, and if her heart wasn't exactly buried with him, there was still an empty ache in her chest.

Ignoring the thrilled chatter of her friend, Beth grabbed an old newspaper that had advertised the contest. Kane O'Rourke's handsome features and level eyes gazed back from a publicity photo. Irish eyes, she thought idly, direct and accustomed to getting what he wanted.

The whole town would think she was crazy, but there was *no* way she was going on her "prize" date.

Chapter One

Local Woman Says "No" To Date With Billionaire.

Kane O'Rourke stared at the bold newspaper headline with something close to horror.

"I'm going to kill him," he growled.

"Kill who?" asked his public relations manager as she walked into his office.

"Your brother."

"He's your brother, too," Shannon said flippantly. "But which one, and what has he done to annoy you...this week?"

Kane glared. "Patrick. He conned me into that damned contest for his radio station. I didn't want to do it, I *told* him I didn't, now look at this." He thrust the paper at Shannon.

His sister lifted an eyebrow. "You're the one who said 'anything you want' when he asked for a favor. When you found out what he wanted you should have just said no. But instead, you still think we're children you have to manage.''

''That isn't it at all, but I know the station isn't doing well,'' Kane said, exasperated. ''So when Patrick asked me to...oh, forget it.'' His family was always accusing him of playing daddy and interfering with their lives, but he was the oldest and he was only taking care of them. ''Just read the article.''

She looked down at the paper. ''You've been turned down? She seemed more amused than offended, and he glared again.

''Not funny. Do you realize how embarrassing this is for both me *and* Patrick's station?''

''You could propose to the lady, maybe that would make her reconsider.''

His eyes narrowed. ''That isn't funny. I'm not getting married, *period*—I've got enough problems. And you aren't helping. Brat,'' he added.

Her lips still twitching, Shannon tossed the newspaper back at him. ''Go talk to her. She looks nice enough. Maybe she just got engaged or something and the newspaper thought it was a better story this way.''

Kane glanced down at the picture of Bethany Cox. He couldn't tell much from the grainy photograph, but she didn't look like a kook or fanatic, and she had a sweet expression. From what the article said, she appeared to be the kind of woman who could understand how important this was for his brother. Patrick had made some mistakes in the past, and now he had a real chance for success...a success he wanted to earn for himself *without* the help of someone else's money.

''I'd probably blow it,'' Kane muttered. ''You should go.''

Shannon laughed and shook her head. ''In the first

place, you're the one who always thinks he can fix everything, so fix this. And in the second place, any woman worth her salt would be furious if you sent a flunky, instead of coming yourself.''

"You're not a flunky, you're my sister."

"Same thing in a case like this." After a moment Shannon leaned forward, her face growing more serious. "Kane, be careful. You're right about it being a public relations problem for the radio station. If she's getting married, I can use it to our advantage. If not, you better talk her into going. Be charming. What single woman would turn down a date with a charming billionaire bachelor?"

Kane folded the newspaper into his briefcase. The picture of Bethany Cox gazed up at him and he grinned ruefully. "I don't know, but I think I'm going to find out."

Beth dug her hand trowel into the soil of her flower bed, her free hand tugging at a particularly stubborn weed. Not a weed, she thought silently. A lovely wild buttercup, which just happened to be in a place she didn't want it.

A car pulled up to the curb, but she wasn't expecting anyone, so she kept pulling at the pervasive plant.

"Miss Cox?"

The roots gave way abruptly, peppering Beth with dirt. Brushing it away from her T-shirt and shorts, she turned her head and saw a pair of legs wearing an expensive pair of suit trousers. She looked higher and her eyes widened.

Kane O'Rourke.

She'd seen him from a distance, of course. On podiums, giving speeches, accepting awards, that kind of thing. But never this close.

"Uh…yes?"

Kane extended his hand. "How do you do? I'm Kane O'Rourke, and we're supposed to go on a date together."

Date?

Together?

Beth blinked. Hadn't he seen the headlines? She hadn't meant it to be such a big deal, but a reporter from the local newspaper had blown everything out of proportion. Honestly, what was so earth-shattering about turning down a date?

"Miss Cox?" He was still holding out his arm and Beth groaned silently. Her fingers were grimy from working in the garden, she couldn't possibly shake hands like a normal human being.

"Sorry, you don't want to touch me, I'm a mess." She wiggled her fingers in the air and started to get up.

"That's all right." Without warning he caught her hand in a firm grip. "Let me help."

He was strong. She had barely enough time to gather her legs under her before being swept upward, and Beth caught her breath as she found herself eye level with Kane O'Rourke's chin. At nearly five foot eight inches she was accustomed to being close in height to most men, but O'Rourke obviously wasn't most men.

She tipped her head backward again.

There was no doubt about his magnetism—intense blue eyes, black hair, an unmistakable air of command, and an underlying sensual quality to his mouth. Beth swallowed, more aware of Kane O'Rourke than she'd been of any man since Curt had died.

"Is there something I can do for you, Mr. O'Rourke?" she asked, trying to pull her hand free.

"It's warm here in the sunshine. Some water would be nice. And a chance to talk."

Talk. Beth could guess what he wanted to "talk" about. Okay, maybe she should have told him personally that she didn't want to go on the date, but you couldn't just call up a well-known billionaire and chat with him. Lord knew, she'd tried.

"Okay," she said cautiously.

"Shall we go inside?"

"Sure."

He finally released her hand and Beth turned quickly. Her skin tingled and her breath was a trifle short, which annoyed her. She wasn't a child to go weak-kneed at the sight of an attractive man. She was a grown woman of twenty-six and had a reasonable amount of experience with the opposite sex—at least enough experience to teach her better sense than she was currently showing.

O'Rourke followed her up the steps and into the house. It was cool inside, the windows open to allow a cross breeze from Puget Sound.

"This is nice," he murmured from behind her.

Beth shrugged. She knew the house was small and old and must seem insignificant to a wealthy man like Kane O'Rourke, but it was more than she'd ever dared dream about having when she was a kid growing up in foster homes. It was *hers,* not someone else's, and that made all the difference in the world. "It suits me."

"I mean what I say, Miss Cox."

The quiet statement startled Beth and she turned. He watched her steadily and she realized he must have sensed her disbelief.

"Of…course," she said. For the first time in years, warmth burned in her cheeks, though she couldn't have explained why; she didn't have anything to be embarrassed about. So she didn't want to go on a date with him. Big deal. She motioned to the breakfast nook. "Please sit down. Would you like a glass of sun tea? I made some fresh this morning."

"That sounds good."

Her heart was still beating unevenly and she drew a breath to regain her composure. Nothing had prepared her for Kane O'Rourke or how perceptive he seemed to be. She should have realized he'd be like that; a man didn't make a mountain of money by being dull-witted.

Trying to appear outwardly calm, Beth scrubbed her hands before getting the pitcher and a tray of ice from the freezer. She carried two glasses to the table. With efficient motions she filled the glasses with ice and poured the tea.

"Sugar?" she asked, and congratulated herself on that single, cool word.

"No, thank you." He was still watching her and amusement flared in his blue eyes. "You don't trust me, do you?" he asked casually.

Beth nearly dropped the pitcher. "What?"

"You distrust me. Do you distrust everyone, or am I special?"

"I trust plenty of people," she snapped, shooting him a look of active dislike. "And I don't have any reason to distrust you. I'm sure you're a very nice person."

"But you don't want to go on a date with me."

Whoa. He certainly believed in being direct.

"Look, I'm not dating *anyone* right now, so it isn't you. I just…"

She lifted her hands, then dropped them helplessly. It was too personal to explain that she'd only dated a few times since Curt's death—each one a complete disaster. She'd had the great love of her life; things like that didn't happen twice, and she wouldn't take second best.

Sighing silently, Beth handed Kane a glass. "I hope you like mint in your tea, Mr. O'Rourke. I grow it in the backyard."

"Sounds great."

Kane kept his gaze fixed on Bethany Cox. She had one of the most expressive faces he'd ever seen. Not really beautiful, but expressive. Her entire body was expressive, from the tilt of her head to the defensive posture of her shoulders.

She was slim and leggy, with small, high breasts and a fall of dark blond hair, gathered together in a messy braid. Not his type, but appealing in her own way. And her eyes were glorious—the shade of warm, gold-shot brandy; he could spend hours watching the play of emotions in those fascinating eyes.

And he knew without a doubt that Bethany Cox wasn't going to be easy to deal with. Between her stubborn chin and the way she'd instantly tried to retreat behind a polite facade, she practically screamed "difficult." He normally avoided difficult women in his personal life—it was complicated enough without the aggravation.

Damn. Why couldn't she have said she was getting married instead of "not dating"?

"Please…call me Kane," he said, trying to give her a charming smile. At least, it was the smile his youngest sister said was charming, though it didn't seem to be having any impact at the moment. "And may I call you Bethany? Or do you go by Beth?"

"It's Beth, but I don't see any point to being on a first name basis since we'll never see each other again." Her chin lifted an inch.

Patience. That's what he needed.

Beth Cox might be royally stubborn, but he didn't think she intended any harm; there was something straightforward and honest about the way she looked at him.

"Who knows, we might end up being friends," he said slowly.

"No, I don't think so." Beth shook her head.

Kane lifted his eyebrows. He'd practically invited her to become part of his life and she was saying no. No seemed to be the woman's favorite word, he thought with wry annoyance.

No to a date.

No to friendship.

No.

He'd gotten spoiled over the years; he wasn't used to hearing no. From anyone.

But *why* was she saying no? Beth Cox was young and apparently unmarried, surely she must have been interested in the prize to enter the contest. And he'd recognized a healthy flash of awareness in her brandy eyes when they'd first met, so she wasn't completely disinterested, no matter what she might say.

"You sound pretty sure about that. Is there something you don't like about me?" Kane asked.

"N-no."

"Then why?"

Her shoulders lifted a scant inch, then dropped. "Let's just say I'm not in your league. Look at you, wearing an expensive suit on a warm Saturday afternoon. I mean, it's *Saturday* for heaven's sake, and you look like you're going to a funeral.'' All at once Beth bit her lip. ''Uh, sorry. It's a very nice suit.''

''A funeral? That's a fine thing to say.'' Kane scowled, trying to decide why he was still sitting in a strange woman's kitchen, getting insulted. Okay, so he was wearing a suit. The fact that his own family had taken to calling him a stuffed shirt did not mean he needed someone else accusing him of the same thing.

Still, he had to admit that compared to Beth, in her comfortable T-shirt with the Mariners' baseball team logo on it, he must seem pretty stuffy.

''I'm really sorry,'' Beth said, sounding genuinely penitent. ''But you asked, and I didn't think before I opened my mouth. Curt used to say it was my biggest fault.''

''Who's Curt?''

Her eyelids flickered, almost imperceptibly. ''My... fiancé. He died several years ago in a mountain climbing accident. He was part of a search and rescue team, and things went bad.''

''I'm sorry.''

''Anyway,'' Beth said quickly, ''I'm sure I look like a wreck to you. It just shows we live in two different worlds.''

Accustomed to feminine wiles and not-so-subtle demands for compliments, Kane's gaze narrowed thoughtfully. But if Beth was fishing for a compliment she had to be the greatest actress in the world. He couldn't help being intrigued—it had been a long time since he'd met a woman who wasn't trying to impress or beguile him.

''You look fine. In fact, you have the right idea.''

Kane unbuttoned the jacket of his suit and shrugged out of it. He heard her swift intake of breath and cocked his head. "Something wrong?"

"Of course not," she said quickly.

The color in her eyes shifted, turning dark, all traces of gold erased, and Kane sighed. She seemed to be in her mid-twenties, which made her ten to twelve years younger than himself. Perhaps he made her nervous, and that's why she'd decided to refuse her prize. Or it could be the loss of her fiancé, though it had happened a while in the past.

"Miss Cox—Beth," he said after a moment. "If you're worried about the arrangements for the trip, I can assure you there have always been plans for separate hotel suites. It's very respectable and aboveboard. Both KLMS and I have a reputation to maintain."

"Heavens, I never thought *that,*" she said quickly. "I'm the last woman you'd ever be interested in...in that way."

I'm the last woman...

Frowning, Kane shook the ice in his glass. He didn't understand her vehement denial. Most of the women he knew had an invincible confidence in their ability to attract a man.

"Why do you say that?" he asked finally.

She lifted her shoulders in another small shrug. "Your taste in women isn't any secret."

"You don't seem the type to read the society page, or what passes for it around Crockett."

"No, but people talk." Beth looked down at her faded T-shirt and shorts. She wasn't the "type" for a lot of things. She didn't really mind, but she was re-alistic—she was far from pretty, and even Curt had looked at more generously endowed women with appreciation. Kane O'Rourke was accustomed to dating the most beautiful women in the world; she'd look ridiculous standing next to him.

Kane lifted her hand and she shivered. Her skin was stained and rough from working in the garden all morning, yet compared to his hard fingers, she felt small and delicate. It was an ironic contrast, especially with a man she'd expect to have professionally manicured nails and soft hands from pushing paper for a living.

"Maybe I *am* a little stuffy, but I'm a decent guy," he said quietly. "My family will vouch for me. You can phone them if you'd like. Of course, my brothers and sisters will probably claim that I boss them around too much." Kane gave her a self-deprecating smile. "I'm the oldest child, so it's an occupational hazard. My sister, Shannon, says I'm not always right—I just think I am."

I'm the oldest.

Beth's heart gave an odd lurch. She would have loved being part of a large family—youngest, oldest, or in the middle, it wouldn't have mattered. "How many in your family?" she asked.

He grinned. "Four brothers and four sisters. And my mother, but she thinks I'm perfect. Naturally."

"Naturally," Beth echoed, though she'd never known her own parents, never known what it was like to have a mother think she was perfect. But she was compelled by the warmth in Kane's face and voice, a voice that held a trace of Irish brogue. She remembered his parents had immigrated from Ireland shortly before he was born, which probably explained the accent.

Kane O'Rourke was the epitome of the American dream. Son of poor immigrants, skyrocketing to success and fortune with the speed of a meteor. Not only that, he'd done it with a widowed mother and all those brothers and sisters to support. And he was so handsome it took her breath away.

Stop.

All at once Beth shook herself and pulled her hand free from Kane's grasp. She'd warned herself against his perceptiveness, she should have worried more about his sex appeal. It had been a long time since she'd touched a man in a way other than friendship, and long denied feelings were demanding attention.

"It must be nice, having such a big family," she said.

Edgily she grabbed their two glasses and carried them to the sink. It wasn't that she didn't like the sensations uncurling in the pit of her stomach, she liked them too much. A steady trickle of water streamed from the faucet and Beth tried to focus on it. Another repair in the making. The little house still had its original vintage plumbing and she'd been learning how to do the repairs herself to save money. She certainly didn't need any distractions. Her life was very full. She had friends, a partnership in a local business. Everything she needed.

What she didn't need was Kane O'Rourke upsetting her hard-won peace of mind. Her fingers closed around a dishrag and she scrubbed at a permanent stain on the ancient sink.

"I don't understand why you entered the contest, if you didn't plan on going," he said.

"I didn't enter the contest," she said over her shoulder. "My neighbor entered me. And Carol has been yelling at me for being an idiot ever since I said I wasn't going. Even though she's married I think she has a crush on you."

I didn't enter the contest.

Briefly Kane wondered if he'd just been provided with an escape clause, then decided he wasn't going there. The easiest, cleanest way out of the embarrassing situation was to convince Beth to go on her "weekend date with a billionaire, separate rooms of course," as the radio station had billed the prize. And the next time Patrick asked for a favor he'd get tossed out on his ear.

"Okay, but why didn't you contact me before making your announcement?"

Guilt, followed by irritation, flashed across her face. "I tried calling both the radio station *and* your company, but never heard anything back. Besides, I didn't exactly make an announcement, the reporter just kept bugging me until I finally said I wasn't going."

Damn. He would have to speak with the switchboard. His employees tried to protect him, but this time he'd missed something that really mattered.

"Beth, this is important," Kane said, deciding candor was the only way to make her understand. "To be honest, I didn't want to be a prize on the radio, but my brother Patrick owns the station and he thought it would be a good publicity stunt."

She turned. "Your brother owns the station?"

"Yes. He switched to country after buying it, and they're struggling to find a niche in the Seattle broadcasting market. Prizes are a big deal in radio and he wanted to come up with something different."

"So he decided on a date with a billionaire as a prize?"

Kane wrinkled his nose. "Yeah. You know how it is with families," he murmured. "We find ourselves agreeing to the most ridiculous favors and stuff. Not that going out with you is ridiculous," he added as she stiffened. "But I felt ridiculous being offered as a prize, and now it's even worse having you refuse to go on the date."

"You should have said no."

"That's what Shannon told me."

"Shannon—your sister?"

"Right." Kane cursed to himself, wishing he understood the complex emotions on Beth's face. Usually women were easier to classify, but he didn't know what to make of Beth Cox…or his reaction to her. For some reason he kept looking at her small breasts and slim body far more than the situation warranted. If nothing else, she was too young and seemed far too innocent. He had a policy about innocence—no playing around with someone who could get hurt.

He cleared his throat. "Anyway, having you turn the date down…it's bad for the radio station. I'd give Patrick whatever he needs, but he's determined to make it happen without my money. He got into some trouble as a teenager—after our father died—and he's never really forgiven himself for it. I think this is his way of proving to himself that he's changed."

Beth sighed. "I'm sorry about your brother, but I don't see how me going could make any difference. Just tell him to pick someone else for the prize."

With an effort, Kane kept from exploding. "It doesn't work that way. Advertisers are particularly sensitive to public relations issues, and listeners can be fickle, too. They're already asking questions and wondering if the contest was rigged."

He could tell Beth was troubled by the whole thing; she obviously was a caring person. The newspaper article had said she was active in various local charities— the Crockett Family Crisis Center in particular—so making a donation might convince her it was to everyone's advantage to play along.

"All right," he said slowly. "How about a donation to that crisis center you're trying to get going?"

"A *what?*"

"A donation in exchange for you going on the date." He pulled out his checkbook and began scribbling. Now that he thought about it, this was the best solution for everyone. No matter what people said, money did solve problems, and he had plenty.

"That's ridiculous."

"Not to me," he said in a grim tone. Between the damaging consequences to Pat's radio station and the embarrassment of being publicly refused, he'd be delighted to get the whole thing behind him. "So we'll go on our date, and you can give the check to the crisis center. Just tell them to keep it private," he added. "I've postdated it so it'll look like I made the donation after our date."

Annoyed, Beth looked from Kane O'Rourke's face to the slip of paper he was holding out. "You're trying to buy me off."

"I'm trying to do my best to take care of everyone. Besides, I don't think spending the weekend with me is such a terrible fate." When she didn't move, he put the check on the kitchen table. "We're supposed to go to Victoria next week. I'll have someone call with the arrangements."

He walked out and she clenched her fingers.

"I'm trying to do my best to take care of everyone," she mimicked, thoroughly annoyed. She didn't need anyone taking care of herself; she did just fine on her own.

Beth snatched the check to tear it up—and practically fainted. There were a whole lot of zeroes at the end of the number. It would answer all the money problems the crisis center was having, and then some. Still, men like Kane O'Rourke were too accustomed to getting what they wanted, buying and selling people without a second thought.

The paper crumpled in her fingers and she dashed onto the porch as Kane O'Rourke reached the end of the walk.

"Mr. O'Rourke, you're forgetting I didn't say yes."

He walked back to the porch. "You want more money?"

"You...*oh*. You just snap your fingers and expect everyone to go along. Well, I am not one of your employees, and I'm not doing anything I don't want to do."

Kane barely kept from grinning. Beth was like a rumpled kitten with its hackles raised, practically spitting in his face. He might not be used to hearing no, but their date would be anything but boring.

"You'll go," he said confidently. "You're intelligent and you care about the community. In the end you'll decide the money will do too much good and that it's worth a weekend to get it."

She let out a wordless shriek. "You're an impossible, arrogant, overbearing tyrant."

"Yeah, but I'm a lovable tyrant," he agreed mildly. His family had accused him of tyranny too many times for it to bother him now.

"I could just keep the check and not go," she threatened.

This time he laughed. He couldn't help it. Beth was the first spice he'd encountered in longer than he cared to remember; he'd forgotten how exciting it was to have someone—other than his family—defy him. In simpler circumstances they might have become friends, but he lived in Seattle, she lived in Crockett, and his life was too crazy for normal people.

"You should take me seriously," she warned.

"I always take women seriously. Besides, I have good instincts about people, and my instincts say you're too honest not to go on our date."

She looked ready to argue, so Kane leaned close and gazed into her brandy-wine eyes. He was having trouble remembering he shouldn't kiss her. Honestly, he couldn't understand why she interested him so much. He'd known plenty of women more beautiful and better endowed than Beth, but none of them had gotten to him so quickly—at least not since he was an overeager teenager with a thirst for curvy cheerleaders in tight sweaters.

He tugged on the end of her braid. "Someone will be in touch, Beth. With the arrangements."

Her chin lifted a fraction of an inch and a devilish expression crept into her eyes. "Call yourself. I have no intention of being 'staffed-out.' If I hear from anyone but you, the deal's off."

She meant it, too, and admiration stole through Kane. Beth was holding a check for a pretty sum in her hands—enough money to solve a truckload of problems—and she still had the nerve to lay down terms.

Damned, if he didn't like this woman.

Chapter Two

"I didn't know you were *that* charming," Shannon announced as she walked into Kane's office late Monday morning and threw a newspaper on his desk.

Kane sighed. "I've seen it."

Another bold title, this time with art.

Billionaire Charms "No" Into Maybe?

Beneath it was a picture of him looking intently into Beth Cox's face, his hand hovering in the vicinity of her chest. To say the least, it was highly suggestive, because you couldn't tell from the photo that he was reaching for the braid that tumbled over her shoulder. His only consolation was knowing the article had been printed in the Lifestyles section of the newspaper, rather than the front page.

The buzzer on his desk rang and Kane pushed the intercom button. "Yes?"

"Mr. O'Rourke, there's a Miss Cox here to see

you.'' His assistant's voice held a wealth of amusement and Kane groaned to himself.

Great. Not only were his employees laughing their heads off, but Beth had to be upset about the invasion of her privacy. Not that he blamed her. He didn't enjoy the notoriety that accompanied his success, either. All too often there were photographers in places meant to be private, and prying questions from people who didn't have any business knowing the things they were asking.

"Tell Miss Cox to come in."

His sister grinned broadly. "I can't wait to see this. A woman with the guts to tell Kane O'Rourke 'no' has to be something else."

"Shannon, leave or you're fired."

"You won't fire me, you practice nepotism, remember?"

She didn't leave and Beth walked in, her face stormy. "It wasn't good enough to hand me a big check, you had to set everything up with a photographer and newspeople to save your pride."

"That isn't what happened."

"Sure it isn't." She flung a handful of confetti at him. "Keep your money. We don't need it that badly."

Kane rounded his desk, instinctively realizing he had to deal with her on a more personal level. The truth was, he should have called the minute he saw the newspaper article, but he hadn't known what to say. Or how she'd react.

"I swear, I didn't know there was a photographer out there. I was leaving the house—how would I know you'd follow me?"

Beth hesitated. He looked sincere. *Darn.* All her life she'd struggled with a tendency to overreact. She'd thought it was under control, then she'd seen the newspaper and come unglued. Maybe she should have thought things out before charging into Seattle and making accusations.

"Much as it pains me to say this, I believe him," announced the woman sitting on the couch.

"Who are you?" Beth asked, though she hardly needed to ask—the resemblance to Kane was unmistakable.

"Shannon O'Rourke," the woman said. She rose gracefully and stuck out her hand. She nodded her head toward Kane and gave Beth a comradely grin. "That big goon is my brother, and I'm his public relations director. Please don't be too hard on him, he's had a rough week. It isn't easy being publicly turned down for a date."

A groan came from the "big goon," but he didn't say anything, apparently accustomed to his sister's lack of respect. Beth stared at Shannon and wondered if everyone in the O'Rourke family was gorgeous, sophisticated, and larger than life. She was a small town girl; she didn't know anything about designer suits and silk blouses.

"I didn't intend it to be public," Beth said finally. "But the newspaper sent someone out and they kept asking questions. I finally said I didn't plan to go and the reporter made a big deal of it."

"Which is exactly what they did with that picture…taking it without us knowing," Kane interjected. "Let's have lunch and talk it over."

"Great idea," Shannon said enthusiastically. "I'm starved."

"You're not invited. Besides, didn't I just fire you?" he asked.

Beth's jaw dropped, but Shannon just laughed. "Don't worry, I get fired at least once a week," she said. "It was nice meeting you. We'll have to get together some time and share horror stories about my brother. He can be a pill, can't he?"

"Brat. You aren't helping," Kane growled.

Shannon waved an unconcerned hand and strolled from the room, leaving a faint trail of expensive perfume. It was obvious from Kane's expression that he adored his sister, no matter how much she exasperated him, and Beth swallowed a pang of envy.

What would it be like to belong like that?

The thought wasn't new and she impatiently shoved it away. She'd learned a long time ago that wishing for the moon was pointless.

"Would you like to eat at the Space Needle, or someplace else?" Kane asked. "McCormick and Schmick's has great seafood."

The question brought her back to earth in a hurry. "There isn't any need for lunch. I'm sorry for over-reacting."

"You have to eat."

"I'm not dressed to go out. I'll get something later."

"You look fine, but we can eat here in the office if you prefer. It'll give us a chance to discuss plans for our trip to Victoria, and you did insist I talk to you directly." Kane lifted the phone. "Please have that deli place deliver a couple sandwiches to the office…yes, the usual for me." He covered the receiver and looked at Beth. "Any preferences?"

She tried not to roll her eyes. The man didn't listen to anything that didn't go the way he wanted. It was probably a good way to make money, but she wasn't so sure about friends.

"Swiss cheese and turkey," she said, plunking herself down on the couch.

Apparently they were going to eat lunch together whether she wanted to or not, so she might as well eat what she wanted. He hung up the phone after uttering a terse order to rush the delivery.

"You always get what you want, don't you?" Beth asked thoughtfully.

"Not always," Kane protested, then a sheepish smile crossed his face. "Well, most of the time."

She couldn't help being charmed. In a single instant he'd disarmed her, which was quite an accomplishment considering how angry she'd been over the newspaper. Her life was pretty ordinary; she wasn't used to having her picture in print, or having people whisper and gossip about her.

What had really set her off that morning was the crowd of women visiting the Mom and Kid's Stuff clothing store she co-owned. Her partner had laughed and said it was good for business, but the loaded questions and raised eyebrows made Beth uncomfortable. And she had to admit, she was suffering from a shred of wounded pride—everyone was surprised Kane had made such an effort to change her mind. She certainly hadn't felt like explaining it had nothing to do with her, and everything to do with saving his brother from embarrassment.

"So, am I forgiven?" Kane asked.

Beth shrugged. She might be charmed, but she wasn't letting him off that easy. "I'm thinking about it."

"You're a tough little cookie, aren't you?"

Though he plainly didn't mean anything by the comment, she stiffened. A kid raised in indifferent foster homes either got tough, or didn't survive. Over the years she'd learned to stick up her chin and never count on anyone. The only time she'd let down her guard was with Curt, and when he died she'd been wounded more than she'd ever imagined possible. Curt had pulled her out of her protective shell, making her that much more vulnerable when the world fell apart.

She couldn't let it happen again.

"Yeah, I'm tough," she muttered. "And don't you forget it."

Confusion replaced the teasing look in Kane's face. "What did I say?"

"Nothing."

"I don't believe that."

Exasperated, Beth glared at him. "What's wrong with you? In polite society when people say 'nothing' you're supposed to pretend it's really nothing and start talking about something else."

"Is that what I'm supposed to do?"

"Yes. Absolutely."

Kane chuckled, grateful Beth's bleak expression had been replaced with irritation. He wondered if she realized how much her face reflected her emotions. A man might not always understand what was going on inside her head, but he'd have an interesting time guessing.

"My family calls me a human steamroller," he said. "But they don't understand."

"Ever think they might be right?"

"I just like to get things done—efficiently, without wasting time. There's nothing wrong with that."

She rolled her golden-brown eyes in disgust. "Not unless you're the one getting flattened with all that efficiency."

"I don't flat—"

A knock on the door interrupted his defense, probably saving him from annoying her all over again. Really, he didn't understand why people like Beth and his family were so stubborn about things. He had more money than he'd ever be able to spend, why shouldn't he take care of their problems?

Their sandwich order was brought in and Kane suggested they eat at his desk. He tried to get Beth to sit in his chair because it was more comfortable, but she gave him another one of her are-you-crazy looks and sat where she wanted.

"I can't believe you eat regular deli food," she commented as he handed her the container with her turkey and Swiss. "Isn't this a little mundane for a billionaire?"

He lifted an eyebrow. The day they had met she'd implied he was stuffy, now she seemed to think he lived an extravagant lifestyle. "What? You think I eat caviar and drink champagne all day?"

Beth munched on a Greek olive and shrugged. She wore a green sleeveless blouse and skirt that emphasized her slim waist. Her small breasts didn't make much of an impression under the blouse, but he had an overwhelming interest in finding out how they would feel in his hands...which was exactly the wrong thing he ought to be thinking.

Odd, he'd dated some of the most beautiful women in the world, but he'd never had so much trouble keeping his thoughts respectable.

"If I'm not at a business lunch or dinner, I mostly grab a sandwich and let it go at that," he said in a gruff tone.

"You're kidding."

He smiled ruefully. "Nope, that's my glamorous life."

"Hmmm." Beth opened her tub of coleslaw and took a bite. She didn't want to like Kane, but she did. Of course, he was far too controlling and overbearing to be the kind of man she'd normally be friends with, but they only had to rub elbows until the weekend was over, and then she'd have the money to give the crisis center.

That is... *if* he wrote the check again. She'd torn the first one into pieces for effect—just another example of her going too far and too fast.

As if reading her mind, Kane dusted his fingers and pulled his checkbook from his pocket. "I should write you another check," he said.

"Uh...okay."

He seemed secretly amused about something, which annoyed her all over again. It was one thing to decide she could put up with him for a weekend excursion, another to actually *do* it. He wrote out the check and she hastily put it in her purse. Even if the money was for a good cause, she was still being paid off.

"If it's all right with you," Kane said. "I've arranged for the limousine to take us to Port Angeles on Saturday morning, where we'll take the ferry over to Victoria. We'll do some sight-seeing, stay the night at the Empress Hotel and return home Sunday afternoon."

She gave him a funny look. "Why not drive ourselves?"

"The contest rules said we'd go by limo. My brother thought it would sound more exciting to the contestants."

"I don't care about the rules. It's too extravagant."

"The station is footing the bill. Patrick insisted. He's stubborn about things like that."

"But—"

"Humor me." Kane chomped down on his sandwich. He obviously didn't enjoy being thwarted, even on something so minor. Maybe he hoped to use the time in the limo to work, since cell phones and laptop computers made it possible to do anything, almost anywhere.

It couldn't be easy for a busy billionaire to drop everything for a weekend in Victoria, especially with a woman like her. If she was sexy and exciting like Julia Roberts or Marilyn Monroe it might be different and he wouldn't mind so much. But she wasn't.

Beth sighed, unaccountably depressed.

It wasn't as if she actually wanted Kane O'Rourke to like her that way, even if her body was all for the idea.

"Beth?"

She realized he'd said something and she'd been too distracted to hear. "What?"

"I asked if you have any particular likes or dislikes I should know about. That is, about restaurants or things to do?"

"Anything is fine."

Kane's eyes darkened to the color of midnight. "A little cooperation would be nice. This is a two-day date, and I want you to enjoy it. We should plan things you're interested in doing."

Beth put down her plastic fork and shoved the remains of her sandwich and coleslaw to one side. "Let's get something clear, this isn't a date, it's…it's…"

He looked amused again. "It's what?"

"Well it's nothing like a date," she snapped. "I'm

only going to Victoria to help the family crisis center, and you're only going to help your brother. That's all."

There. She'd established the ground rules. Kane couldn't possibly think she had any interest in him as a man, and she'd made it clear she knew he wasn't interested, either. There wouldn't be any embarrassing misunderstandings to make the weekend uncomfortable.

That is...any *more* uncomfortable.

Because even if her head and heart weren't interested, her body had gone over the fence. You would think after everything she'd experienced in her twenty-six years—including the death of her fiancé—she wouldn't respond to such an unsuitable man. But Kane O'Rourke was so gorgeous he was knocking her hormones on their heels.

"Look," she said. "I have to go back to work."

"Yes, to your store in Crockett."

Beth blinked. "How did you know about that? Did you have me investigated?"

Shaking his head, Kane motioned to the newspaper laying on his desk. "That last article was very thorough." He waited, then let out a breath. "You do know there'll be photographers going with us to take pictures in Victoria? Maybe even a television crew. The whole point of the contest is publicity for Patrick's station. And I'll have to announce you've decided to go after all, so you might have reporters bothering you again."

She rolled her eyes. "Like they ever stopped?"

"Er...right. I'll walk you down to your car."

"No," Beth said hastily. "I'm fine."

He ignored her, of course, and all the way down to the parking garage she was aware of curious glances from Kane's employees. He didn't seem to notice and she wondered how you ever got used to being the center of attention. It was probably something that happened gradually, until you didn't even realize that everyone was watching.

As Kane held the car door for her, he smiled. "I'll see you Saturday morning...we need to leave by six to be sure of catching the ferry."

She forced a smile of her own. "Great. Six sharp. Do me a favor, though."

"Sure."

"Don't wear a suit."

Kane laughed as Beth pulled from her parking space. To his surprise, he was actually looking forward to the weekend. There were worse things than spending time with a woman who wasn't marriage hungry and anxious to score with a man simply because he had a hefty bank account.

In the meantime he had a hell of a lot of work to do. Somehow, the more money he made, the less freedom he seemed to have. Weekends were just two more days to get things done, and taking one off would mean lots of catching up.

He couldn't even remember the last time he'd had lunch without reading reports at the same time—it seemed a waste to just eat when he could be getting something done.

Still, it was rather nice eating with Beth like that. Between her stubborn attitude and that blasted contest she should have been a thorn in his side, but it wasn't turning out that way.

The alarm went off at five on Saturday morning and Beth opened a bleary eye. "Shut up," she growled.

The clock kept blaring and she stuffed a pillow over

her head. She didn't like morning at the best of times, but especially not after failing to sleep more than a couple of hours the night before. Then the phone rang, joining the noise from the radio. Beth moaned and grabbed it, succeeding in knocking the radio to the floor. It made a squawking noise, then fell into blessed silence.

"Yes?" she mumbled into the receiver.

"You're still in bed, aren't you?"

"Uh...Emily."

It was her business partner at the clothing store. They got along great except for her being one of those annoying morning people who woke with the sun. Of course, she had incentive—a husband who worshiped the ground she walked on, along with a darling daughter and another baby on the way. Most of the time Beth managed not to envy Emily, but for the last several days she'd found her heart aching more than usual.

It didn't make sense, because she didn't want something from Kane. She just wanted...something. Beth dropped her head back on a pillow and wondered when her comfortable life had become inadequate.

"Yup, it's me," Emily said. "You have to get up, you have one hour to make yourself beautiful for Kane O'Rourke."

Beth made a face. "That would take more than an hour, it would take a miracle."

Her friend sighed. "You're a very attractive woman."

"Says the woman with the face of an angel," Beth retorted. "I'll talk to you when I get back."

Putting the phone down, Beth pushed away the blankets, yawning and stretching, relishing the cool morning air on her bare skin. She'd already packed an overnight bag; it waited in the living room.

Padding into the bathroom, she glanced into the mirror. Her nipples were drawn tight, crowning her barely B-cup breasts. "A little cleavage would have been nice," she murmured. Overall her figure wasn't awful, but it certainly didn't inspire any great male fantasies.

She'd barely been touched by a man, even during her brief engagement. It was her own fault. Curt had wanted to make love, but she'd been determined to "do things right" with a traditional wedding night. Now she wished they had made love a hundred times. At least she'd have something to remember...something to distract her from thinking about Kane O'Rourke.

"At least I'm a natural blonde," Beth said, lifting her chin. Dark blond, to be sure, but blond. Not that Kane would ever see the proof of it.

When the doorbell rang fifty-five minutes later she was just finished swiping mascara on her lashes. She grabbed her purse and overnight bag and hurried to the door.

"I'm ready," she said, flinging it open.

Kane waited, one hand holding a bunch of flowers, the other tucked into a pair of jeans. She stared, breathless at the difference casual clothing could make. A white shirt emphasized his shoulders—shoulders that seemed even more broad and muscular now that they weren't covered by an expensive suit. He looked younger, more relaxed, and altogether sexy.

"Is something wrong?" he asked, taking the bag from her fingers.

"Yes. I mean, no. Nothing."

He held out the flowers and she tore her gaze from

his face and took the bouquet. It was a surprising mix of small yellow roses and daisies. "Thank you."

Beth locked the door, her heart racing even harder. Kane O'Rourke in a suit was enough to make a woman think twice about all kinds of things; in a pair of jeans he could make serious inroads on her principles. Especially carrying daisies.

The bouquet did make her wonder, but it was probably just for publicity. At the thought, a thread of sadness crept through her. She loved flowers, but Curt had been the practical sort who didn't go for romantic gestures—or else she just didn't inspire that kind of thing.

At the curb sat a black limousine. Behind it idled a Chevy Blazer, black also. A photographer was filming them from an open window and her cheeks warmed. It had to be the newspeople Kane had warned her about earlier in the week. The opulence of the stretch limo made her grateful for the early hour since her neighbors would still be in bed—a hope that was dashed when she saw a curious face peer from the house across the street.

Swell.

She waved and scrambled into the vehicle with more haste than grace, sinking into the butter-soft leather seat. She put the flowers to one side and pushed her hands into the cushions, trying to sit straight.

"This is ridiculous," she muttered.

Kane handed Beth's bag to the chauffeur and climbed in next to her. "What's ridiculous?"

"Spending this kind of money on a car."

He hid his smile. "There's nothing wrong with a little luxury. Besides, it gives us time to talk."

"Oh, yeah, that's a great idea. Like we have anything in common to talk about."

"We'll find something." Kane stretched his legs out and rolled his shoulders. He suspected Beth was one of those people who got up a little irritable in the morning, which unfortunately led to thoughts of the ways he could find to wake her up in a better mood.

He wouldn't be taking it anywhere, but it was baffling the way she made him feel. Beth Cox was too young for him, too innocent and too damned much trouble.

So why did he have this urge to spend the next seventy-plus miles kissing her senseless?

Chapter Three

"I can't believe we're actually taking a limousine to Victoria," Beth said as they climbed to the passenger deck of the ferry. "Talk about conspicuous consumption."

Kale shrugged. "It's easier to have someone drive us around the city. But if you want, we can walk off with the foot passengers, rather than ride the limo."

"You mean, in company with our chaperons?" She cast a significant glance at the camera crew toting equipment along behind them. They were lagging behind, struggling with their load on the steep and rather narrow stairway.

"Hey, I warned you there'd be photographers."

"As if I had any choice in the matter."

He chuckled, knowing there was a shred of truth in what Beth had said. She could have turned down the money for her charity, but he wouldn't have stopped until he'd found a way to change her mind. It was one thing for him to be embarrassed by a newspaper article, another for his brother's business—and pride—to be hurt, however innocently it might have happened.

They walked to the bow of the ferry and stood with excited passengers as the ferry chugged away from the pier. Seagulls screamed and dove above them with impertinent challenges, and as the boat made its way around the breakwater, the breeze picked up and the sea became choppier.

Beth leaned on the rail and gazed into the horizon, a far-off expression on her face. Gradually the cold early-morning wind off the Strait of Juan de Fuca drove their fellow passengers inside, leaving them alone on the deck—alone except for the stubborn camera crew, who had set up a discreet twenty feet away. At least they didn't have to worry about every word they said being recorded.

"Aren't you freezing?" he asked finally.

"No, but you don't have to stay outside because of me," she murmured.

Kane rested his elbows on the rail next to her. "I'm fine, but I'm wearing more clothes than you are."

"Is there something wrong with my clothing?" Beth asked, her head tilted in challenge.

"Nope. You look terrific." His tone grew a little husky and he hoped she'd put it down to chilly wind and noise from the ferry engines. The cold air was doing what a lover's hands would accomplish, puckering her nipples beneath a thin green T-shirt. White shorts cupped her trim bottom, the cuffs a respectable three inches above her knees, and a pair of sandals emphasized the slender length of her legs.

There was nothing obvious or overblown about Beth, just an understated elegance he'd never fully appreciated before in a woman.

"So tell me," he said, forcing his gaze out to the blue-green water of the Strait and away from temptation. "You never explained what was so terrible about us going on a date together."

"I told you, this isn't—"

"A date," Kane finished for her. "I know. But it doesn't matter what you call it, you still said 'no.'"

Beth rubbed the back of her neck and then her arms, as if she'd suddenly become aware of the bite in the air. "My life is settled, I don't need contests and fantasy dates to make me happy."

Interesting. Kane suspected she wasn't being entirely honest with herself, or with him. Most people wanted *something,* even if they didn't know what that "something" might be.

"*Are* you happy?"

She flashed him an angry look and planted her hands on her hips. "That's none of your business."

"Shhh." He put a finger over her lips and motioned to the camera crew. "Some of those folks are from a local television station. It isn't good press for them to see us fight—at least it wouldn't make the kind of press my brother needs."

"Mmm." She angled her head backward and gave him a sweetly false smile. "Would it make good press if I bite your finger?"

Kane laughed. Beth was bright and sassy like one of his sisters; he only wished he could think of her that way. Like a kid sister. Nothing sexual or uncomfortable, just a nice woman who didn't confuse his body.

Hell, it was his own fault. He'd been celibate too long, buried in his work and bored with the whole social scene. A man got to a certain age and he didn't feel like playing games with women, watching them dance around, hopeful he'd decide they were the perfect billionaire's wife. They didn't realize the money wasn't important, it was only a means to an end.

With money you could take care of your family and protect them. Without it you were helpless.

He still remembered what it felt like to be nineteen, one minute on top of the world, the next minute seeing it fall apart. Remembered the crushing pain of suddenly losing his father, of looking at his mother and brothers and sisters, fearing he wouldn't be able to hold everything together.

A seagull swooped low and hovered for an instant, catching their attention before it swooped away again with a shrill cry.

"He's saying we're crazy," Kane murmured.

"For going to Victoria, or for going together?" Beth asked pertly.

"You don't give up, do you?" he asked, more curious than annoyed. "You didn't want to do this, and you aren't going to give it a chance. At the very least we could pretend we're friendly. That isn't much to ask, is it?"

She sighed and gathered her windswept hair away from her face. "I'm just uncomfortable. I was never very good at dating or anything, and since Curt's accident…" Her shoulders lifted and dropped. "There doesn't seem to be much point."

Curt.

The fiancé who died in a mountain-climbing accident—or to be more precise, the fiancé who was killed while trying to rescue someone. It was strangely daunting to wonder about the contrast between himself and this other man. There weren't many heroes in the world, yet Beth had been engaged to one.

Kane searched her face, trying to tell how much pain the memory brought. "How long ago did it happen?"

"Almost five years." The distant look filled her eyes again. "It's not like my life hasn't gone on. I miss him, but he loved me and wouldn't want me to stop living because he isn't here."

"But you don't think you can fall in love again...or that you'll ever get married?" Kane frowned. "That isn't right."

Abruptly she turned back to the water, so all he could see was her profile. "And that's an interesting observation from a man who openly tells the press *he's* not planning to get married," she drawled.

A low chuckle surprised Beth and she glanced at Kane.

"What's so funny?"

"Just the thought of two determined singles being pushed together like this. Don't you see? It makes things perfect. We can do some sight-seeing, have a nice dinner and enjoy ourselves without worrying about any wayward expectations. With that in mind, you'll be happy to know I changed our reservations from the 'romantic attic suites' at the Empress Hotel, to regular suites."

Romantic attic suites?

"That's a relief," she said, without being entirely sincere.

Emily had told her about the Empress Hotel after staying there with her husband, and deep down Beth felt a pang at missing the "special attic rooms." According to Emily, romantic was an understatement. They were beautiful and private, decorated with the Empress's original antique furniture, including some four-poster and canopy beds. Beth had never slept in a genuine four-poster bed, but she thought it would be fun.

More fun for a honeymoon or wedding anniversary, but she wasn't likely to have one of those.

"So, are we okay?" Kane asked.

Beth shook herself. He was worried about the publicity angle of their "date," and she was still worried about him thinking she had silly expectations.

"Sure," she said. "I'm sorry about being so sensitive. It's just everyone has been speculating about this romantic date with you, when all along I know it isn't the least bit romantic. I mean, if you really think about it—what's romantic about going out with a perfect stranger?"

Kale threw back his head and laughed. "You really *are* innocent, aren't you?"

"What's that supposed to mean?"

"Most people are strangers until they get to know each other…which is usually through dating."

An embarrassed warmth crept up Beth's neck and she wrinkled her nose. "You know what I mean."

"Do I?"

He was being difficult, which should have annoyed her. Unfortunately she was too aware of Kane at the moment to be annoyed, at least for something so minor.

"I mean a date between two people who have never met and have no basis for attraction," she said as severely as possible.

"Ah." Kane leaned closer until his arm touched hers, a startling warmth in contrast to the brisk wind off the water. "There's no basis for attraction, then. Between us?"

"Of course not."

"I'm a man, you're a woman. That seems pretty basic."

"I said *basis,*" Beth hissed, a fraction of an instant before she saw the teasing light in his blue eyes.

Jeez.

"Shannon was right," she said. "You're a pill."

"That's just the little sister talking. You know how families are."

"Not especially. I was raised in foster homes—no relatives at all, as far as I know."

From the defiant tilt to Beth's chin, Kane guessed the reaction to her childhood hadn't always been good. It was hard to imagine having no one at all. Bad as it was when his father died, he'd still had the rest of the family.

"Is that why the crisis center is so important to you?" he asked softly. "Sometimes I think people who don't have families appreciate them more than those who do."

Beth twisted a strand of hair around her finger and shrugged. "I love being involved, but I'm not a crusader or anything. There's nothing dysfunctional about wanting to help."

"I know." Kane let out a breath. They'd gotten into much more personal territory than he'd ever intended, it wasn't any wonder she was defensive. "Speaking of help, what do you say to a hot cup of coffee? I'm sure I could persuade one of our camera-toting chaperons to get some for us."

"I'm sure you could," Beth said in a dry tone. "But let's get it ourselves and save them the trouble."

Sunlight poured through the windows of the ferry, so there was enough light for Kane to wear his sunglasses in the building. If they weren't recognized it would be easier.

It was warm inside, with children laughing and running and a babble of conversation rising above the steady throb of the ferry's engines. The line at the snack bar had thinned, and they selected coffee, along with muffins, then found an empty table.

The coffee was terrible, but it was hard to mind when Beth gave him a sleepy smile and rested her chin on her hand.

"I'm sorry for being touchy," she said. "I'm not a morning person."

"I kind of figured that."

"Do you always get up early?"

"Mmm." Kane pushed his cup to one side. "Usually no later than five. I work out and get to the office around seven."

Beth shuddered. "Five a.m.?" She made it sound like the middle of the night. "I love to sleep late. That's real luxury, you know, staying curled up in bed until late in the morning. Especially on a winter day, when it's cold and stormy outside."

The small amount of caffeine he'd consumed hit Kane's system on overdrive. He *knew* she wasn't trying to be suggestive. As far as Beth was concerned she'd dispatched the question of them being compatible in any way. She was just talking, completely comfortable with their status as disinterested strangers. Unfortunately he wasn't as disinterested as she thought.

And he suspected her own feelings weren't entirely neutral, though she'd given him little enough evidence.

If only she wasn't so much younger and so obviously inexperienced—the two were an impossible combination for the sort of sophisticated affair he'd enjoyed in the past.

He cleared his throat. "You like stormy days, huh?"

"I like listening to the rain." Beth let out a self-conscious laugh. "The truth is, I'm not a very complicated person. I enjoy simple things the best, like reading or hiking in the mountains, or working in my garden."

It had been a long time since Kane had done anything simple, but it suddenly sounded very appealing. He didn't have time for hiking or gardening, and his reading was consumed by analyses and reports and dozens of memos, yet Beth's words conjured an irresistible image of peaceful mornings in bed, leisurely loving, and time to think.

Dangerous thoughts for a man who worked fourteen hours a day, and even more dangerous to consider whose face had popped into his head as a bed partner.

"Don't you ever sleep in?" Beth asked.

Kane could tell she wanted to say something more, maybe even suggesting he slow down a little. "Never," he said quickly. "I guess I'm too compulsive."

"That's too bad." She popped a piece of muffin into her mouth and sipped her coffee, then looked at him suspiciously. "We don't have to get up early tomorrow, do we?"

"Nope, you can sleep as late as you want."

She let out an obvious sigh of relief. "That's good. I'm not sure I could do 5:00 a.m. twice in a row."

"I think you could do anything you put your mind to," Kane said sincerely. "As my mother puts it, 'ye've got steel in your backbone—but don't forget to bend every now and then.'"

"She sounds nice...and very Irish."

"That she is," he agreed, his own accent becoming more pronounced. His mother had survived more than any woman ought to go through, yet she remained a faithful member of her church, a devoted parent—and tireless nagger about him slowing down. She deserved a comfortable life, though she wouldn't accept a fraction of what he wanted to give her.

"Have you ever been to Ireland?"

He shook his head. "Shannon goes with mother every year, but I haven't had time. Someday, maybe."

A thoughtful frown creased Beth's forehead as she ate the last of her muffin. She neatly folded the cupcake paper holder inside a napkin and wiped a small drop of spilled coffee from the table. The gesture suited her, and Kane recalled the simple, tidy decor of her house.

"I don't understand," she said finally. "You have all this money, and hundreds of employees to take care of things. How could you not have time to travel?"

"I've been busy *making* the money."

Her eyebrows lifted. "Okay. When will you have enough?"

The genuine puzzlement in Beth's face made Kane pause, and he sensed a void opening in front of him. He had more money than he could ever spend, yet he'd never once considered slowing down. No matter how much his mother nagged, or his brothers and sisters teased, he just kept pushing.

Why?

How much money was enough to make him feel the family was safe? And why, of all the people who had asked how much money was enough, should it be Beth who made him feel as if he'd been struck in the face with the truth?

No.

He was overreacting. He couldn't remember the last time he'd done something frivolous like spend a weekend sightseeing. It wasn't Beth, it was the circumstances. Anyway, she couldn't understand. Her fiancé was gone and she didn't have any family, so her priorities were different.

"I…it isn't just the money," Kane said. "I built the business, I'm not going to abandon it just to enjoy myself. A lot of people depend on me for jobs." The excuse sounded lame, even to him, but it was the best he could do.

"Is that what taking a vacation means to you? Abandoning your business?"

"I'll go someday," he said in a tone that meant the subject was closed. His employees understood that tone perfectly, and made themselves scarce on the rare occasions they heard it.

"Not if you drop dead of hypertension or a heart attack first," she murmured. "What good is a gazillion dollars if you're six feet under?"

Obviously Beth wasn't one of his employees.

An announcement came over the loudspeakers, telling car passengers to return to their vehicles since the ferry was coming into dock.

"Mr. O'Rourke?" said one of the camera and video crew. They'd been sitting on the other side of the ferry, having been asked to clear the aisle by one of the ship's officers. "It's time for you to go below."

"Go ahead. We'll be down in a few minutes. Or we may decide to walk off, rather than take the limo."

"But Mr. O'Rourke, we're supposed to cover the entire date," the man protested.

Kane was already tired of having a media chaperon,

and knew Beth couldn't be enjoying it, either. "I told you to go ahead," he snapped. "You don't have to take pictures of us walking down a flight of stairs or going through customs." The one good thing the news crew had done was stay far enough away for Beth and him to talk privately.

"Oh, my *God*," a woman shrieked all at once. "I knew I recognized them. They're that couple—the billionaire and his date. She said no and he charmed her into it."

Damn.

The next thing Kane knew cameras were flashing, and pens were being thrust in their faces for autographs, no one was paying attention to the loudspeaker and the second reminder to go below to the car deck. The only blessing was seeing the news crew jostled into the background by eager tourists.

Beth had a frozen smile on her face as she signed her name on a dozen different scraps of paper.

Patrick had done a good job of advertising the weekend in Victoria; it seemed as if everyone had heard about it. And what fascinated them most was the idea of a woman turning down a date with a billionaire. The way things had turned out, Patrick had gotten a whole lot of free publicity because of Beth's original decision not to accept her "prize."

"Why did you do it?" demanded the woman who had recognized them. "He's gorgeous and rich. Jeez, how could you refuse to go?"

Beth swallowed and drew a breath. She liked people, she just didn't enjoy being the center of so much excited attention. "My neighbor entered me in the contest, so I wasn't really expecting…you know, to win.

I guess I wasn't thinking straight." It wasn't the real reason, but they didn't need to know that.

Chuckles rose from the group, accompanied with jokes about not appreciating her luck and "looking a gift horse in the mouth." Beth sneaked a look at Kane, wondering how he felt about being called a "gift horse." She was starting to understand how humiliating her public rejection must have been, but to her surprise, he didn't look insulted, just frustrated.

"Ladies and gentleman, please," exclaimed a ferry official as he elbowed through the throng with a couple of helpers. "If you'll come with me, Mr. O'Rourke. And you, too, miss. I think it would be better if we get you both off first."

Forcing her way through a crowd of people wasn't Beth's idea of fun, but she clutched her purse and inched out of the seat. Kane reached out with one arm and clamped her tight to his side. A shock of awareness spun through her body, distracting her from more immediate concerns.

"Take it easy," he murmured. "You'll get used to this."

"W-what?"

"The attention. It goes with the territory. It'll be better once we get off."

"Right." With an effort she kept color from flooding her face. Crazy thoughts about Kane had spun around her head, which was totally illogical. But his words had conjured an image of permanence.

You'll get used to this.

Sure.

Like she'd ever get used to being asked for her autograph and having her picture taken by strangers, much less in a single weekend. Or that she even *wanted* to get used to it, which she didn't.

The ferry had already docked and another team of crewmen were blocking the exit. Kane and Beth were allowed past the rope barricade, then the ship's crew began explaining, over the other passengers' objections, that they would have to wait.

"What do you think the camera crew and chauffeur are doing?" Beth asked as they approached the custom's official.

"I really don't give a damn," Kane muttered. "Maybe we can get a few minutes of peace this way. We'll see them at the hotel later. That'll be soon enough."

Customs took only a few minutes, and they hurried from the building. Beth drew a breath of fresh, sweet air and looked around happily. It had been a couple years since she'd come to Victoria, a town people called "more English than the English." She didn't know if it was true, but the city was beautiful—from the grand parliamentary buildings up from the docks, to the trailing baskets of flowers hanging from the old fashioned globe and wrought iron light posts.

"Let's get down where the camera crew can't see us if they drive by," Kane suggested. "The longer we're away from them, the better."

Beth nodded and they hurried down to a lower walkway that skirted the water of the quaint harbor. Whistles and shouts from the ferry behind them caught their attention, and she saw they were in view of the foot passengers waiting to disembark. Though some distance away, it was plain they were still interested and snapping pictures.

"I feel bad we got special treatment getting off,"

Beth said, biting on her lower lip. "You may be used to it, but I'm not. We should have waited our turn with everyone else."

"It wasn't exactly special treatment, more like a safety precaution," Kane replied, a devilish smile on his face. "But we could give them something to make up for it. A reward, so to speak."

"Like what?"

"Like this."

Putting a hand on Beth's waist, Kane tugged her flush against his body. He gazed into her wide eyes and felt her breathing quicken. A flush of triumphant satisfaction filled him. Beth Cox definitely wasn't as indifferent as she pretended. He shouldn't be glad about that, but he was.

"I think a kiss would reward them nicely. They'll be convinced they're seeing a real romance developing between us."

She flicked the tip of her tongue over her lips. "Are they supposed to think that's exciting?"

"That depends on whether you kiss me back, or slap me."

"You don't think a slap would be exciting?"

He hesitated, nearly saying it wouldn't be exciting for him, not nearly as much as a kiss. But it was exactly the wrong thing to say, particularly when he'd gone to great lengths to assure Beth that he knew their date wasn't really a date.

Except…it sounded like a date, felt like a date, and was making him feel like a kid on a date. Not a deadly dull dinner date at one of Seattle's most expensive restaurants, but an honest to gosh date with a girl, where he didn't have a clue about the outcome.

For the first time in longer than he could remember, he was having fun.

"Play along, Beth," he whispered. "Give them an eyeful."

With a mischievous smile, she wound her arms around his neck. "Like this?"

"Exactly like that." His voice was hoarse again, but hell, she was doing things to his blood pressure he'd thought were no longer possible. Putting his mouth over hers, Kane tasted the sweetness of the muffin she'd eaten, and the lingering flavor of coffee.

On Beth, the terrible coffee didn't taste so bad.

In fact, it tasted great.

He was tempted to deepen the embrace, but they were in a very public place. No matter what he'd said about giving the ferry passengers a reward for having to wait, he wasn't an exhibitionist. Quite simply, the kiss was about finally getting a chance to touch Beth.

Still...he lingered another few seconds, savoring the sweet innocence of her mouth, before lifting his head.

"That—" Beth cleared her throat. "That was interesting." The swirl of emotions in her eyes was too complicated to sort out.

"Then you're glad you didn't slap my face?"

Her enigmatic smile drove a fresh surge of heat through him. "I haven't decided."

"Let me know when you make up your mind."

"Oh, you'll be the first to know, Mr. O'Rourke. Don't worry about it."

Chapter Four

"So, what's next on the agenda?" Beth asked brightly...just as if they weren't still holding each other in a loose embrace that made Kane feel as if he'd been sucker-punched.

"You did say what you wanted to do, so we scheduled a visit to Butchart Gardens," he said, reluctantly dropping his arms. "Then we return and have high tea at the Empress Hotel. I think lunch is supposed to happen somewhere in the middle."

"It would be more fun to just wander around on our own," Beth said.

A slow smile grew on Kane's face. "You mean ditch the news crew altogether and make this more like a real date?" He winced the moment the words "a real date" passed his lips, expecting Beth to explode. "Uh...but we need to catch up with the limo," he added hastily.

"Who needs a limo?" She grabbed his hand and headed down to the marina. "Let's buy a bus tour of the city. It'll take us out to Craigdarroch Castle, along the waterfront...lots of places. They also have tours that go out to the gardens.''

"What's Craigdarroch Castle?" he asked.

"A nifty old house."

There were plenty of old houses in Seattle, and Kane had never enjoyed visiting historic sites that much to begin with, but he let Beth pull him along. "Why is it called a castle?"

"I don't know. Maybe because it's got lots of rooms and turrets and looks like one."

It sounded like a good enough reason to Kane, and much easier than thinking about that kiss. He was long past the time when he analyzed and reanalyzed a kiss, wasn't he? A man reached a certain point in his life and didn't wonder what things like that meant, or endlessly second-guess himself about how it should have been handled.

Right.

And he was an idiot, because he *was* second-guessing himself. But there was something about the sweet freshness in Beth's face that made him feel younger than he had in years...maybe younger than he'd felt since his father's death.

They waited at the light to cross the busy street in front of the Empress Hotel, an impressive structure that stood like a sentinel in front of the quaint harbor. The city was a feast for the senses with its frosted cake buildings, hanging flower baskets and gaily dressed tourists.

Just then he spotted the news crew heading toward them, followed by the stretch limo.

"Uh-oh.''

He grabbed Beth's hand and hurried her into the crowd still crossing the other street.

"The bus tour place is the other way," she protested.

"Yeah, but we're going to have company if we're not careful."

Beth peeked through the hubbub of tourists and saw the limousine and black Chevy Blazer for herself. One of the frustrated reporters was leaning halfway out the window, scanning the people streaming in every direction. Fortunately he was focused toward the hotel and not at them.

Laughing, she took the lead and they raced to hide behind the carillon tower. Kane leaned over her, one hand resting on the concrete tower wall, a broad grin splitting his face. Her heart skipped a couple of beats.

"The museum is right here," she murmured. "It might be a good time for a visit."

His brow wrinkled attractively. "I thought we were going to the castle. We can get a taxi, rather than going on a tour. Then we'll plan out the rest of the day."

Beth shook her head. She didn't know a great deal about Kane O'Rourke, but she had an idea of his life— all schedules and work and carefully planned days.

"We don't have to plan anything. We're in front of a great museum, let's go inside."

Without waiting for agreement, she headed for the entrance. After a moment she felt a strong hand at the small of her back and smiled faintly. Kane might learn to be more spontaneous, but he'd never forget to be a gentleman. She'd never been around a man like that, someone whose old-world manners were as second nature as breathing.

He paid for their entrance to the museum and they rode the escalator up to one of the upper floors. Though it had been years since she'd visited Victoria, the Royal British Columbia Museum was a dear friend to Beth, and she took Kane to her favorite display first—the recreation of an old town, complete with train station and silent movie theater.

"Isn't it great?" she murmured, standing in the train station with her eyes closed, feeling the vibration through her shoes as the "train" roared down the tracks, whistle blowing. It was an illusion, but she loved it.

Kane gazed at Beth, more intrigued by the look on her face than anything the museum had to offer. A part of her had slipped away, lost to the threads of a younger time woven through the exhibit. What would happen if he kissed her again? Would it bring her back?

With an effort Kane deliberately stepped farther away. He needed to see Beth with clinical detachment. This *wasn't* a date. He didn't have any right to kiss her. They weren't a couple, and never would be.

It was hard to remember though, when they later sat in a darkened exhibit area and listened to the stories behind the displayed tribal masks. The recorded voice and Native American music cast a haunting spell across the listeners. When Beth wiggled in apparent discomfort, Kane slid off the upholstered lounge seat to the carpet, pulling her along with him. She tensed, then relaxed against his chest.

Yes.

He crossed his arms over her stomach and held her securely between his bent knees. It put Beth's head conveniently close so he could kiss the curve of her neck. Which he did, the soft fragrance of her skin an enticement he couldn't resist.

"Kane...don't," Beth's faint protest could barely be

heard above the melodic voice recounting the creation story of Raven and the clamshell.

"Just making you comfortable," he whispered in her ear.

Of course, it was making him quite *un*comfortable, in a completely masculine way. Desire, hot and insistent rose behind Kane's zipper, and he counted to a hundred. It was an exquisite pain, all the more so because he certainly wouldn't find release. Even if Beth was willing, he wouldn't start an affair with reporters hot on their trail. Some women didn't care about their reputations; he didn't think she was one of them.

Other visitors drifted in and out, but they stayed— anonymous and ignored—listening through several of the story cycles. It was curious, feeling so much at peace, while at the same time feeling ready to explode. The calm lasted until a large group of schoolchildren came in, chattering and asking questions from their teacher.

Without a word Beth slipped from his arms and they drifted into the main section of the First People's exhibit.

Only when their stomachs began to rumble did they leave.

"I'm sure there's a restaurant at the Empress," he said as they stepped into the sunlight.

"Yeah, but we can also get a hot dog and have more time to see stuff."

She was serious.

"You don't want a nice lunch?" *Something expensive with deferential waiters and fine china.* The women he usually socialized with would insist on that kind of luxury.

"Hot dogs are nice."

"Sure," he said, unconvinced.

Beth smiled, though she didn't feel the least like smiling. She shouldn't have kissed Kane, or talked about such personal things on the ferry. Her common sense had clearly flown the coop. Kane O'Rourke was charming and thoughtful, and if she wasn't careful she could fall for him in a big way.

A chill went through her that had nothing to do with the cool breeze sweeping in from the water.

She didn't want to fall in love again. It was too damned painful. Besides, Kane was out of reach. An enormously wealthy man with a normal family, as far from her circumstances as he could be. So maybe an informal, happy-go-lucky lunch of hot dogs wasn't such a great idea.

"All right, we'll go to the hotel if that's what you want," she agreed.

Kane nodded, which she supposed was best. He might eat nifty deli sandwiches at the office, but he'd want something fancier in other circumstances.

Somehow, it was easier to keep thinking about Kane as if he was just a spoiled rich guy who didn't know how regular people lived.

Perversely, the minute Beth had agreed to a sit-down lunch at a restaurant, Kane wanted the hot dog she'd suggested. Something had happened in the space of a second. One minute she was filled with laughter and spontaneity, the next a shutter had come down over her face.

He cleared his throat. "A member of my staff came over and registered us at the hotel yesterday, so I have our keys. Why don't we take a look at our rooms, and then decide."

"That sounds fine."

"What's wrong?" he asked bluntly.

"Nothing, I said it was fine."

She gave him a bright, artificial smile and Kane gritted his teeth. The woman was impossible, but that didn't stop him from wanting her in the worst way. And it didn't stop him from wanting her to change back to how she was acting just minutes before, with a real smile on her face.

Of course, he liked challenges. So maybe if he just considered this another challenge, then it would be all right. In the back of his mind Kane vaguely realized there was a flaw in his reasoning, but he wasn't thinking clearly when it came to Beth Cox. He was getting an odd sensation around her, a sense of being at sea without a lifeboat.

While Beth checked out her suite, he made a few calls and set up a private lunch…with some very special additions to the usual room service. When everything was ready he invited her to see his own sitting room.

Beth walked in, stared for a few seconds, then burst out laughing.

The room had been hastily banked in ferns and flowers, and spread out on the plush carpet was a red-checked picnic tablecloth. A giant plastic "ant" was peering into a basket filled with hot dogs in buns. A formal waiter stood at attention, linen napkin over his arm, holding a frosty cold bottle of sparkling apple cider.

"You sure know how to treat a girl right," she said, still grinning.

"Anything for a lady," Kane declared. He took the

cider from the waiter and handed him a large denomination bill. "We can take it from here."

"Very good, sir." The waiter left, though not before scooping up the plastic ant. "Three's a crowd," he said, giving Kane a wink.

Beth sat cross-legged on the tablecloth and shook her head. "I'm glad you didn't go to a lot of trouble," she murmured dryly.

"I just made a phone call. By the way, they're hand-cranking ice cream for us down in the kitchen."

"Really? I didn't think they made hand-cranked freezers any longer."

He shrugged. "They made sure they found one in order to get that bonus I offered."

"It must be nice to have that kind of money," Beth said, yet she didn't sound envious.

A thoughtful frown creased Kane's forehead. The sensation he'd felt earlier came back stronger, the feeling of being out of his depth. It was ridiculous. Beth was so young, how could he feel uncertain around her?

Maybe because you have nothing she wants, the voice whispered in Kane's head, but he ruthlessly pushed it away. There had never been time for second-guessing himself. He just put his head down and did what had to be done.

The hotel hadn't brought the plastic picnic cups that he'd ordered, so he poured the cider into crystal champagne flutes and handed one to Beth. "To friendship," he said.

Faint surprise registered on her face as she clinked her glass with his and sipped the contents. "But we're not friends," she said after a moment.

Kane leaned back on one elbow, more comfortable than he'd expected to be sitting on the floor. "I'm wearing jeans, not a suit. The day we met you seemed to think it was one of the reasons we couldn't be friends. Actually that's the only reason you mentioned. Of course, you were a little embarrassed for insulting my suit.''

''It was a nice suit.''

''Nice for attending a funeral—isn't that what you suggested?''

Beth took a bite of hot dog and chewed for a long moment. Even if Kane was teasing, she didn't know how to respond. She'd reminded herself to keep a distance, but he'd already shortened that distance with his ''picnic.'' How many wealthy men would eat simple, ordinary hot dogs in the private suite of an exclusive hotel?

She carefully spread pickle relish on what was left of her hot dog. ''What's wrong with accepting we're two very different people, without anything common except the need to get through this weekend?'' she asked.

Kane's lips tightened. ''I didn't realize spending time with me was such an imposition.''

She chomped down on the end of her hot dog, trying not to grit her teeth. Men were men, no matter how much money they had. ''It isn't, it's just that...'' Her voice trailed and she shrugged.

He couldn't understand. Kane O'Rourke had probably never been afraid in his entire life. He had everything: a big family, security, love. It was easier to take risks when there were people who cared about you. The one risk she'd taken had ended up hurting her so badly she'd barely survived.

Everything about falling in love was a risk, but she could hardly explain that it was her attraction to Kane that was the problem. He'd either think she was crazy, or get paranoid that she was trying to catch herself a wealthy husband. Which was ridiculous, and anyone looking at them would agree. He was a magnificent, glossy-feathered eagle and she was the brown wren that had strayed into his territory.

Meanwhile, Kane still looked aggrieved and she sighed again. "You're a great guy," she said, trying to sound observant, rather than admiring. "But you have to be honest—I'm the last person you would have chosen to share a weekend with."

"I'm not so sure about that," Kane muttered. "You're fun to be with when you aren't being so prickly."

"I'm not prickly."

"Of course you are. And iron maidenish, too."

"I absolutely am *not* an iron maiden. That's a terrible thing to say."

"Yeah, but you insulted my suit."

"Do you even know what an iron maiden is?" Beth demanded. "I mean, aside from being the name of a heavy metal rock band. Which, I'm sure, you've never even heard of."

He shrugged, seeming wholly unconcerned, and she pushed at his shoulder, wholly irritated. She might not be in his league, but she wasn't chopped liver, *or* an iron maiden or whatever he meant by it. She pushed harder and a moment later he flipped her so she ended staring up, as he stared down at her.

Lurking in the back of Kane's electric-blue eyes was laughter, and a touch of something she didn't want to understand.

"K-Kane?"

Her cider had splashed over both of them, and his

gaze traveled with a drop of cold fluid as it rolled down her jaw. Her own eyes drifted shut as Kane dropped his head. An instant later the velvet warmth of his tongue caught the droplet and slowly retraced its path.

"Mmm. Tastes good," Kane breathed. His fingers threaded through her hair as he found other golden drops of juice and flicked them away with the tip of his tongue.

Beth shivered.

The lazy, sensual warmth did funny things to the pit of her stomach. It was as if he had all the time in the world to sip those bits of sweetness into his mouth. She hadn't known that a man could be so maddeningly patient in getting to a kiss. And she had no doubt Kane was going to kiss her; everything from his arms bracing him above her, to the tension in his strong body, told her what he wanted.

She'd just decided to protest when Kane settled his mouth over hers. His tongue darted inside, traced the edge of her teeth, then delved deeper.

All thoughts of protest vanished.

It had been so long, and never like this. She couldn't remember being kissed so thoroughly, so gently, every cell of her body melting from the slow mating of mouths. Kane's hand skimmed her arm, grazed the side of her breast and slid into safer territory at her waist. For some reason it was more erotic, wondering where he might touch her next, than if he'd actually offered a more intimate caress.

Beth's legs moved restlessly. It was odd, the way she felt. Sort of awful and wonderful at the same time.

"Easy," Kane whispered.

His weight settled over her and the solid power of his body relieved some of the strange quivering in her veins. He was so much larger she should have felt smothered and overwhelmed, but she didn't. It felt right, and filtering through the pleasure was a hint of panic.

"Kane? I don't think…that is, maybe…umm…" Her words trailed.

"Easy," Kane urged, dropping small kisses down Beth's neck. He didn't want her thinking too much—thinking led to stopping, and stopping led to questions. He definitely didn't want any questions, especially the soul-searching variety.

The knowledge that she could catch fire so quickly filled him with both delight and a nagging guilt. Delight, because he knew it was genuine. Guilt, because he was stoking a fire his conscience wouldn't allow him to put out. Beth was a virgin, he had no doubt of it. Taking that from her wasn't an option.

Yet he groaned when her fingers gripped his shoulders. He wanted those fingers all over him, touching and teasing and making him crazy. He'd forgotten how great it felt to get crazy now and then.

Why did Beth affect him this way?

It didn't make sense. She was attractive, but he'd met hundreds of attractive women. And she wasn't overly endowed. Yet her small breasts burned against his chest, reminding him of what his father used to say when he was sixteen and chasing after buxom cheerleaders.

Anything more than a handful is just a waste, son.

Kane had never quite agreed with the comment, now he thought his father might be right. Beth made up a sweet handful, and his right hand began inching upward to check it out when another of Keenan O'Rourke's quotes popped into his mind.

Go slow with a lady, they're the ones worth keeping.
Swell.

He lifted his head and stared into her turbulent face.

"Don't you dare apologize," Beth said before he could say anything.

He was glad he'd waited. An apology was exactly what he'd planned to offer. "What should I say?"

"I don't know, just don't apologize."

"Uh, well, I shouldn't have let it go that far."

"That's it. I've had it."

Beth gave him a shove. She didn't have a fraction of his strength, but he obliged her by rolling away. With any luck she wouldn't notice he was still aroused. Honestly, he couldn't remember the last time he'd been so undisciplined.

"I've tried to give this weekend a chance like you asked," Beth said. "But I don't have to put up with that."

Kane rubbed the side of his face. He was probably lucky she hadn't slapped him, though he didn't have a clue why she was so angry. God, women were unpredictable. "Put up with what?"

"Stupid male superiority about men being responsible for how far things go, and having to handle things for poor little women who have no self-control."

"That's not what I said."

"Huh."

Beth gritted her teeth. She liked Kane O'Rourke, which scared the bejeebers out of her. But she wouldn't have gone to bed with the man, or even gone any further with that kiss, because she had better sense than to play with dynamite.

"For your information, I was trying to put the brakes on when you stopped," she hissed.

It was true. She'd grabbed his shoulders to inject some calm into the situation, but he'd distracted her with a kiss in her cleavage…her *small* cleavage. Actually she didn't really have a cleavage unless she was wearing one of those Wonder bras, though she tried to believe she had one the rest of the time.

Blast.

Beth sat up and righted the basket of hot dogs.

Okay, so she'd have to be more careful for the rest of the weekend. Falling head over heels into infatuation with one of the wealthiest men on the planet wasn't an intelligent thing to do. Kane would likely laugh his head off at the idea, and *she* would be taking a risk she wasn't prepared to handle.

So, from now on, it was hands off.

For both of them.

"It doesn't matter," Beth said, clasping her fingers together just in case she got tempted. Right now it was a toss-up between exploring Kane's chest, or hitting him. "I know it only happened because I'm convenient, but you can go back to your regular social life once Monday rolls around. I'd really prefer not having any repeats of what just happened."

Kane opened his mouth, then snapped it shut. Is that what Beth really thought? That he'd kissed her simply because she was convenient? Or worse, because he was some kind of sex-crazed man who couldn't go without a woman for a single weekend?

He was annoyed and ready to tell her about it…until he saw the flicker of humiliation in her face.

Oh, criminy.

It would just make things worse if he explained that ever since they'd met he'd had an overwhelming desire to kiss her, despite her not being his type. They'd just get into a discussion of type, and he'd feel like a shallow, immature kid for admitting a preference for women with more curves. Of course, that preference didn't seem too important at the moment; Beth had a way of making him appreciate what she *had,* rather than what she didn't.

When he really thought about it, he couldn't quite understand what had always attracted him to top heavy women, anyway. Compared to Beth they were sort of...well, *top heavy.* Her figure was nicely balanced between top and bottom, with hips that were slim, but unmistakably feminine.

"I don't have much of a social life," Kane said calmly. "I'm too busy. And I'd never make a pass at a woman simply because she was convenient. What kind of a man do you think I am?"

"Rich, powerful and able to have any woman you want," Beth replied instantly.

"Obviously not *every* woman."

She pretended not to notice the significant look he gave her. "Do you want another hot dog?"

"That's not what I'm hungry for."

"There seems to be some potato salad in the picnic basket."

Kane fixed Beth with his gaze. "Just in case I'm not making myself clear enough, I would love to spend the rest of the weekend with you, wearing out the sheets in the bedroom. It has a nice king-size bed and an extra firm mattress—which, if you had any experience in that department, you would know is a plus. Anything to say about that?"

Beth swallowed, though she didn't look quite as shocked as he'd expected. "Is...isn't it time for us to head out to Butchart Gardens? I understand they're particularly lovely this year.''

"Don't you want to wait for the homemade ice cream? I'm sure it'll be nice and creamy." He tried, and failed, to keep the suggestive note from his voice. It wasn't as if he was trying to seduce her. Hadn't he already decided it was a bad idea for both of them?

"No," she said quickly. "Definitely not."

He sighed. "That's what I thought you'd say."

Chapter Five

Beth agreed to taking a taxi out to the gardens because it was expedient, and also because it was easier than arguing the point with Kane.

In all honesty, she was rather embarrassed.

She didn't believe he had an undying passion for her, though it flattered her ego to hear him talk about spending the weekend...wearing out the sheets. On the other hand, she wasn't sure where she'd lost control of the discussion. One minute she was justifiably vexed over Kane's arrogance, the next he was turning her inside out with talk about *sheets*.

"Are you all right?" he asked in the seat next to her, looking sinfully handsome and relaxed. "I could still apologize, if that's what you want."

Anger simmered again in her chest, and Beth glared. "I told you—"

"—not to apologize," he finished for her. "But my daddy taught me to be a gentleman, so I wanted to make the offer, just to be sure."

Beth sent a cautious glance toward the taxi driver, who seemed more than a little curious about his passengers.

"I'm fine. Hunky dory. Can't you tell?"

Kane lifted his shoulders, then let them drop. For a man who had gotten hot and heavy a short time before, he sure seemed calm. It was really irritating, though she couldn't say so.

What had happened to her plan? The one where she remained friendly but distant, and cordial but remote? There had been *nothing* remote about kissing him in the middle of the carpet, and it certainly hadn't been distant—you couldn't have gotten a credit card between them during most of that kiss.

Credit card?

Good.

That was best.

She had to think about Kane's money and the fact he was so stinking rich he didn't remember what it was like to be a normal person on a budget. Of course, that only worked as long as she didn't remember his family and that overprotective responsibility he felt toward them. She could see that it might become annoying to have him always charging to the rescue, but it was also nice.

When they arrived she accepted his helping hand from the taxi and tried to look cool, calm and collected. It wasn't a look she was familiar with, so she faked it.

"Er...tell me more about your father," she said. "Do you take after him?"

One of Kane's eyebrows shot upward. It hadn't taken Beth long to put those polite barriers up again. Not that he hadn't seen it coming; she'd been too quiet on the drive, the wheels obviously turning in her head.

"Dad was a hard worker, but he couldn't find any opportunities in Ireland, so he saved and brought the family to America. Mom was seven months pregnant with me at the time."

"It must have been hard to travel when she was so far along."

"Aye, but they wanted me to be a citizen of their new country."

"You sound very Irish at times," Beth said, shading her eyes from the sun and tipping her head backward to look at him. "It's a beautiful country. Did they ever regret leaving?"

His head shook. "My mother sometimes misses her homeland, but the only thing she regrets is that damned accident that killed my father," he said harshly. Even after all these years, the memories of that terrible summer were seared into his gut, and the anger could burst out, just like that, surprising him with its intensity.

"It must have been difficult losing him," Beth said softly. Her voice had lost its cool edge, and was filled instead with compassion.

"He was a logger. I was supposed to be working that summer in the forest, instead I got an engineering internship through the university."

A thoughtful frown tugged at Beth's mouth. "Forestry work is dangerous."

"Yes." His tone was deliberately hard and uninviting. The last thing he'd intended was to discuss his father's death; some things were best left alone. Everyone had their own demon to battle, and his was the lingering guilt that he'd been too ambitious about his chosen career to take a job working with his father. He couldn't have prevented the accident that killed Keenan O'Rourke, but at least he would have been *there*.

"I think he must have been a wonderful man," Beth said, not the least bit intimidated.

"Why?"

She put her hand on his arm. "Because he raised a fine son."

The quiet, certain words were a balm to the ancient scar left from his father's death. He wanted to kiss her again, but instead walked down the path with her fingers drawn through the crook of his elbow. Beth had a way of cutting through things that weren't important. He liked that. And he liked that she didn't give a fig for his money except for the way it could help other people.

Hell.

He definitely had to kiss her again.

It was that or spend the rest of his life feeling deprived, and he wasn't good at deprived.

"I need to kiss you again," he announced.

Beth's footsteps faltered for a moment, then picked up again. "I thought we cleared that up."

"I'm a man. Those kinds of things don't go away that easily."

"Try harder."

Kane thought about the condition of his body, but he couldn't make a crude comment, not to Beth. He could bide his time and get a kiss. It crossed his mind that he wasn't exactly being a gentleman, which made him uncomfortable in a different way, so he shook his head.

The whole thing was probably good for him. He wasn't used to being with women he couldn't have. It was just his money. They acted like it was some type of aphrodisiac and made him irresistible. All except Beth.

A pair of children came down the path, their high-pitched laughter rising in the clear sunny air. Kane and Beth stepped to one side so they could dash by. Their parents followed, all the while calling out to "be careful and slow down."

"I don't know how people do it," Kane muttered.

"What?"

"Raise children. How do they get that kind of time and energy?"

Beth lifted one eyebrow. "Not everyone works eighteen hours a day. Some people have time for other things in their life."

"I don't work eighteen hours a day," he protested.

She gave him a quizzical look and he sighed.

"Maybe I work fourteen hours a day, but that still doesn't leave any time for children."

Or a life, Kane added silently.

Being around Beth was making the absence of a life more obvious. He thought about the way she'd described a lazy morning with the rain beating down, and felt a yearning that he'd never known before. Even her house wasn't cluttered with things, it was quiet and tasteful, just like her.

Beth might be young, but she could teach him a few things about living.

"I suppose *you* want children," he said lightly, only to see some of the amusement fade from her face.

"I used to want a dozen. But that was before…you know."

Yeah, he knew. Before her fiancé died.

"I've thought about taking some foster children," Beth murmured. "Except kids need both a mother and a father, and I can't provide that."

"I think any child would be lucky to live with you, father or not," Kane said sincerely.

The color rose in Beth's cheeks. "Thanks."

"I mean it." He lifted her chin and looked into her golden-brown eyes. "You could do anything you wanted. I don't think I've ever met anyone quite like you."

The compliment made Beth warm all over, but she couldn't be foolish. Kane O'Rourke was a charming man, and compliments were stock-in-trade for charming men. And he'd already proven she was vulnerable to him, so she needed to be particularly careful.

"You...let's go down to the fountain," she suggested, albeit breathlessly. "It's beautiful."

Kane agreed and they drifted down the various paths until they reached the viewpoint for the giant fountain. It appeared to be coming from a natural lake, but it was actually part of the old quarry.

"It's amazing this was once a quarry," Beth mused.

Kane wrinkled his nose. "It was?"

"Yes. Didn't you know?" She leaned on the railing and watched the complicated spray of the water as it rose from the green lake. "The family wanted to beautify the area, so they established the gardens. It's amazing what a little hard work can do."

"And money," he added.

She turned and looked at him curiously. "Do you always think about money first?"

"Sometimes I think about other things."

There was a subtle shift in Kane's gaze and Beth fought the urge to squirm. Her bustline had never drawn much attention, so she didn't know why he'd be interested, yet he seemed awfully preoccupied with that part of her anatomy.

Most likely it was just curiosity, plain and simple. No doubt he'd never been with a woman with so little to offer in the chest department. If he'd gotten a good feel he would have lost interest plenty quick. The thought was depressing, so she shoved it away and flipped her hair away from her face.

"Let's have high tea up at the restaurant. We didn't eat much at lunch and I'm hungry."

A slow smile crinkled Kane's eyes. "About lunch, we—"

"High tea is a tradition in Victoria. It's very English," Beth said quickly, annoyed she'd forgotten and reminded him about…well, *lunch.* It was a Freudian slip. She'd never be able to eat hot dogs again without remembering the feel of his body across hers.

She deliberately kept things light, sipping her way through the tea offered by one of the garden restaurants, admiring the flowers, the landscaping, and keeping things on an impersonal level. When Kane finally said he'd call a taxi to take them back to Victoria, she shook her head and sweet-talked their way onto a tour bus returning to the city.

The late-afternoon sun shone through the open window and she swayed sleepily, listening to the chatter of the over-sixty crowd on board the bus. It was a senior citizen tour group, dressed in golf clothes and the odd straw hat.

"You two married?" asked one cheerful lady with determined carrot-red hair. It was an eye-popping color, especially since she wasn't a day under eighty.

"Uh…no."

"Just dating, so far," Kane said cheerfully, shaking hands with the lady. "But you never know."

"Yes, we do," Beth muttered beneath her breath. "And dating is all there is to it."

The redhead patted her hand. "Never give up hope, dearie. I brought five husbands around to a proposal. And I've got my eye on another." She motioned with her head toward a gentleman sitting in a dignified pose, his hand on a cane. "Ain't he a keeper?"

"He's great," Beth agreed. "But he does seem a bit starched, if you know what I mean. Maybe you'd be better off with someone more easygoing."

"Nope." The woman leaned forward and whispered in a conspiratorial tone. "Those are the best ones in the bedroom. Take my word for it, hon. Once you're alone with them, watch out! I'll bet your fella handles like a stick of dynamite."

With an effort, Beth kept from looking at Kane. A few days ago she would have described him as starched, now she didn't know. The last thing she'd expected was for him to kiss her the way he'd kissed her during their "picnic." Or to say he wanted to do it again.

"We don't know each other that well," she said.

"Sure we do." Kane slung his arm across her shoulder, a devilish expression on his face. "And I've got a short fuse when it comes to Beth."

"Didn't I know it?" the elderly woman cackled. "You look the type. I bet you could have given Elvis a run for the gold, and that man was *fine*."

"Really?" Kane was inordinately pleased. It had been so long since he'd thought much about his appeal to women. He engaged in occasional liaisons, but he couldn't remember the last time it had really mattered. Or if it ever had. As for being attractive, there hadn't been time to think about it since he was a teenager.

"Do I remind you of Elvis?" he breathed into Beth's ear.

She shivered and shifted away as far as the seat would allow. "Elvis is dead."

"The King won't ever die," cried someone from across the aisle.

To Kane's disappointment, the entire bus began discussing Elvis Presley, so he couldn't tease Beth any further…or hear any confessions of breathless attraction to him. Of course, breathless attraction might be a little much to expect, but he was willing to hear any concession. She was a damned stubborn woman. Fortunately she did have some soft spots.

He watched from the corner of his eye while she chatted with the assorted senior citizens and thought about how she'd sweet-talked the driver and group into letting them ride back to Victoria. It was her basic goodness that people responded to, her concern and genuine interest in what they were saying.

By the time they'd arrived in the inner harbor of the city, Beth had collected more than a half dozen addresses and promises to write. The lady with the carrot hair gave him a broad wink as they disembarked, then made her way to the distinguished gentleman she'd singled out as her next husband.

"I think she might actually catch him," Kane murmured, watching the white-haired man break into a smile.

"She might be just what he needs," Beth said. She turned her head and smiled herself, and a crazy thought crossed Kane's mind. Crazy, because it occurred to him that Beth might be just what *he* needed, the sweet and generous spirit lacking in his sterile world of high finance.

But even if he had time for a wife, it wouldn't be fair to her. He was too much older, too tangled in his business, unable to be the kind of man she deserved…too different from her heroic fiancé.

The realization was sobering, though he'd known it before.

"Let's go up Government Street," Beth suggested, tugging on his hand. "I'd like to get some spices and stuff at the tea store."

They joined the stream of visitors mingling on both sides of the busy shopping street. T-shirts were offered at two-for-one prices, and racks of postcards vied for attention with every imaginable souvenir. The sidewalks were so crowded they were jostled back and forth. Kane finally locked his arm around Beth's waist, grateful for the excuse. Aside from her faint start of surprise, she didn't object.

He grinned.

It had been so long since he'd gone shopping for himself, he'd forgotten some of the benefits.

Inside the store, he noted a tea and coffee bar, and suggested Beth select her items while he got them some coffee.

"Tea, please," she said. "Apricot, if they have it."

"They'll have it," he assured firmly.

She gave him a look that said she knew he'd pay extra to get what she wanted, and that it wasn't necessary. "If it's not on the menu, don't make them go to any trouble."

Kane sighed, exasperated. "You just don't appreciate how much money can smooth things along. Why not give it a chance? You might like it."

The laughter in Beth's face stilled and she shook her head. "I'm going back to my own world tomorrow, remember? Besides, money is nice, but there has to be a balance between wanting and getting.''

Kane waited in line and watched Beth wander through the store, looking at some items, shaking her head at a few, and picking up a small selection.

It frustrated him. He could buy the contents of the shop for her and it wouldn't make a dent in his wallet. Why wouldn't she let him do the one thing he was good at?

"Damn," he muttered softly.

The more she turned down the gifts and the luxuries he was accustomed to providing, the more he wanted to give them to her. He liked how unspoiled Beth was, yet how did he handle a woman like that?

"Sheila trouble, is it mate?" asked someone in a heavy Aussie accent.

Kane looked at the man and raised his eyebrows. "Sheila?"

"Lady trouble," he clarified.

"Oh. Yeah, plenty of trouble."

"She belong to you?" the tourist asked, motioning toward Beth.

"Absolutely." Kane nodded, at the same time hoping Beth wouldn't get wind of this particular conversation. She wasn't the type to appreciate the idea of "belonging" to anyone. Of course, women didn't understand the way men talked. It didn't mean they thought they *owned* someone, just that they had rights that other men didn't. Not that he had rights with Beth, but Kane wasn't going to admit it.

"Good luck, mate. She's a right fair Sheila."

"Yeah, she is."

Kane kept his gaze fastened on Beth. The more he looked at her, the more he liked what he saw. Despite the busy day, she still looked great. Her hair was a little rumpled, but that just meant it caught the light better. Her legs were long and slim, her sweet bottom was neatly outlined by her shorts. And it annoyed him to realize another man had immediately appreciated what it had taken him longer to recognize.

He ordered their beverages and arranged to pay for Beth's purchases, then waited at a small table for her to finish.

A few minutes later she came over, her face flushed from an argument with the cashier.

"He said you already took care of this." She motioned with the bags. "I didn't want to go shopping so you'd buy me something."

"I never thought you did."

"Kane, you can't just buy everything for people."

"Why not? I've got to be good for something."

"You..."

Beth sank into a chair and regarded him gravely. Is that what Kane thought? That he had to buy things for people because he wasn't "good" for anything else? It wasn't true, yet it also wasn't as unbelievable as she might have once thought. He'd talked about his father's death and she'd seen the guilt he hadn't admitted to feeling. Maybe he'd gotten the idea that money was the only way he could make up for a sin he hadn't really committed.

"I'd much rather have you carry my bags, than pay for them," she said slowly.

"That's nothing. Of course I'll carry them."

"It isn't nothing, and I knew you'd offer. You're the truest gentleman I've ever met."

"I'm sure that isn't so. Your fiancé must have been pretty special."

She took a sip of her tea. It was apricot, just like she'd asked. "Curt was a fine man, but he was young and sometimes thoughtless." Beth had never admitted it to herself, but it was true. There were times Curt had stomped on her feelings without even knowing he'd done it.

"But he died saving other people."

Beth nodded, her thoughts drifting back to the day of Curt's death. Her world had fallen apart so thoroughly, so terribly, she'd barely functioned for weeks. It had always seemed disloyal to remember the times that weren't so great, but maybe it wasn't. Maybe it was just part of living and loving.

"He was a good man, but not perfect," she murmured. "And I never knew when he'd risk everything to help someone, or just for fun. It didn't matter how chancy it might be. He was a volunteer fireman, as well as being a member of that mountain rescue team. He loved danger."

Maybe more than he loved me.

It was the one thing she couldn't say aloud.

And it wasn't the truth, even if she'd sometimes felt that way. He'd just thought he was invincible and could do it all. In the beginning, his boundless confidence was one of the things she'd found most attractive.

"Danger, huh?" Kane's face was thoughtful. "I can see how that would be hard to live with."

You have no idea.

Once again the question of loyalty rose in Beth's mind. "I...I sometimes wonder if I could have taken it, wondering what was going to happen next," she admitted. "At the time I didn't have any doubts, but now I realize how hard it would have been. Especially after starting a family."

"You would have stayed," Kane said. "You're too stubborn to give up. You would have worked it out somehow."

Beth laughed. "I'm not sure that was a compliment."

"Oh…it definitely was a compliment."

The warmth in his eyes made her swallow. She hadn't intended to invite anything, just to let him know that she saw more in him than just his wallet. A man like Kane O'Rourke didn't need her respect, but it couldn't hurt to know she thought he was a nice guy.

"You're a busy man," she said slowly, "but you helped your brother by agreeing to the radio contest. That was pretty great of you. A lot of people wouldn't have done it."

"I hated being a *prize*," Kane grumbled.

"But you still said yes."

"Of course I said yes. I couldn't say no when Patrick needed something." He looked puzzled, as if *not* helping his family was a concept too foreign to understand. "I told you Patrick got into trouble when he was a teenager. He's really made something of himself, but it hasn't been easy. And he never asks for anything, so I knew it was important. For that matter, the family never asks for anything."

Beth hid a smile at the faintly aggrieved tone in Kane's voice. He'd become the "man of the family" at a young age, with even younger siblings. He'd supported them, helped raise them, and now couldn't understand why they wanted to fly on their own. It was part and parcel of being a parent—the part she'd never looked forward to herself.

Letting go was never easy.

"I know I didn't act grateful about winning the

prize, but I'm glad you agreed to do it,'' Beth said, gathering their cups together and tossing them in a nearby trash can. "I'm enjoying the weekend."

"You are?"

"Yes. And I'm glad you talked me into going."

Laughter grew on his handsome face. "I didn't exactly talk you into it."

She thought about the check he'd given to her, then decided he wasn't talking about the money he'd donated to the family crisis center.

"Right, you browbeat me into going."

"Some people have to be convinced to do what's good for them."

She grinned. "I suppose fun is good for everyone, and I haven't been to Victoria in a long time."

They walked outside and paused a moment, their eyes adjusting to the longer rays of light.

"There's a nice Italian and seafood restaurant not too far from the hotel," Beth suggested when Kane asked where they should have dinner.

"Sounds good."

They returned to their suites and changed, then walked down the waterfront toward the restaurant. Beth was conscious of Kane's warm glances, and for the first time in her life felt really desirable. It was an illusion, of course. She wouldn't compare well to the type of woman he normally dated, but apparently her strapless green silk dress had been a good choice.

"Where do you suppose the news crew is?" she asked as Kane held the chair for her at the restaurant.

"Who cares."

"What about the publicity for your brother's radio station? I'm not fond of reporters, but I can see how it helps advertise the station."

Kane grimaced. "They'll find us in the morning, and I can't think they need *that* many pictures of a man and woman on a date, walking down a street or admiring flowers."

Maybe, but Kane wasn't just any man, and this wasn't just any date—something she was supposed to remember. But it was hard to keep those barriers up. He was far more...*real* than she'd expected. Far more interesting.

Beth was still thinking about it as they took a walk after the meal. There wasn't any moon, and in Thunderbird Park the air had a heavy blackness. Kane had laced their fingers together, and with their free hands they explored the textures of the various carved totem poles, lingering at one Beth remembered was from the Haida tribe.

"It seems to me the Haida had a comfortless view of the universe," Beth said. "But I don't know a lot about Native American cultures—certainly not as much as I should."

Smiling to himself, Kane tugged Beth into the farthest, darkest corner of the small park. "I know something they have in common with everyone else."

"What's that?"

"This."

Dipping his head, he found her soft lips with unerring accuracy. She jumped as he gathered her closer, but she didn't protest. His body pulsed. He'd needed this, needed it more each time Beth touched something deep inside his soul. He just didn't need to think about what it meant, because that would be dangerous.

"You feel so good," he muttered between kisses.

With excruciating slowness, she lifted her arms and put them around his neck. It arched her small breasts into his chest, and he backed her against a solid surface so he could explore their roundness.

Beth sucked in a breath as Kane's fingers circled her breasts. A part of her didn't want him to touch her. It would be incontrovertible proof she was less than generous where other women were better endowed, but she also ached in a way she'd never known. A wonderful, awful, needing ache she didn't understand.

With an expert flick of his thumb, he flipped the silk bodice down and cool air struck her skin.

"Kane?" she gasped, only to be lifted high in the air.

Something velvety and wet flicked over her nipple and everything in Beth's body clenched. He pulled the hardened tip into his mouth, tugging gently one moment, alternating with a strong suckling that sent fire through her veins.

Of their own accord, her legs grasped him around the waist and she grasped his shoulders. The rough texture of wood rubbed into her back as he somehow balanced her enough to pluck her other nipple between his fingers, then rubbed his thumb over the point. She hadn't expected his hands to be callused and hard, but the proof was in the rough, splendid caresses.

Beth's head fell backward in a daze. Through the leafy canopy overhead she saw a single star.

It seemed like the only light in the thick darkness, and she moaned. It had to stop. They couldn't be doing this in a public park, however private it seemed.

Yet it was difficult to remember a reason for stopping when Kane palmed her other breast. It seemed to satisfy him, because a harsh groan came from his chest and the suckling from his mouth became so fierce it almost hurt. He gentled instantly, playing and shaping her with his tongue.

When her legs began shaking so badly she lost her grip, he lowered her to the ground. She lost his mouth on her nipples, but both his hands found them, and he joined their lips in an open kiss.

"Beth. Ah, Beth," Kane groaned finally.

"We shouldn't be doing this," she muttered.

"I know." He rested his forehead against hers, still playing with her breasts in a way that made it hard to think. "You're like candy. So sweet. I've never known anything so sweet."

"I'm glad you...um, enjoyed it."

The sound of voices in the distance made Kane jerk upright. What had he been thinking? It was bad enough to risk his own exposure in the tabloids, another to take a chance with Beth. He fumbled with the bodice of her dress until she pushed him aside and covered herself.

"Same goes as earlier. Don't apologize," she warned shakily.

Kane closed his eyes briefly and prayed that no photographers had caught them. There were ways to take pictures, even in such low light.

"You're right. The same goes for earlier," he muttered. "It was a mistake, I shouldn't have done it."

"Then we're agreed about everything." Beth walked toward the lighted street. She stumbled slightly, and Kane caught her elbow.

"You're mad," he said.

"What ever makes you think that?"

"Intuition."

The park was only a short distance from the Empress Hotel, and Beth held her head up through the elegant lobby and into the elevator. She *was* furious, but it wasn't about being kissed.

Actually she was upset with herself over that part, but furious with Kane and his maddening notions about being responsible and calling it a mistake. In her heart she'd known he'd kiss her again. She could have avoided the evening stroll and going into the dark park.

But she hadn't, and now she'd have to deal with the aftermath. Her body wasn't cooperating with the solitary life she'd chosen. It wanted more. And the worst part was that it wanted Kane O'Rourke, a man she couldn't have on any terms.

Chapter Six

What time was it?

Kane rolled over and blinked at the light coming through the window. It was his penthouse bedroom window, but it didn't look right, somehow.

Rubbing his aching temple, he picked up his watch and groaned.

"I can't have slept that late."

He slumped back and covered his eyes. Actually he barely slept the past two nights. He'd gone over and over Saturday evening in his mind until he was dizzy. Beth hadn't spoken a single word once they'd reached the hotel, she'd gone straight to her room and closed the door with a heavy snap. She'd been equally uncommunicative the follow day. Posing for the cameras, smiling on cue, but treating him with cool civility when they were alone.

Why had he said kissing her was a mistake?

It was, but a woman never appreciated being told something like that, particularly one as innocent as

Beth. He wanted to call her, to make things better, but he didn't have a decent excuse.

Kane rolled on to his back and shoved the pillow from under his head. It wasn't any help remembering that even with the fiasco Saturday evening, he'd had a better time than he could ever recall having. Beth was fun and perceptive, with a wisdom that reached beyond her innocence.

God, she made him feel good. Ten feet tall with the simplest compliment. He didn't know whether to be glad or unhappy that the weekend was over; Beth touched something deep inside him that he'd forgotten even existed. The temptation to see her again was overwhelming.

The doorbell jarred through his throbbing temple, but before he could think about answering he heard the jangle of keys. Since it wasn't the day the cleaning service came, it had to be a member of the family. He would have to collect the various sets of keys floating around the O'Rourke clan; they didn't need access to his penthouse.

"Kane, are you alive?"

Shannon.

He barely had time to drag a blanket over his hips before she burst into the room.

"Oh, good. You *are* alive," she said, not appearing overly concerned. Under her arm were the inevitable newspapers.

"I don't suppose it ever occurred to you that I might be sleeping," Kane growled.

Shannon consulted her watch. "At nine in the morning? Why would that occur to me? Rain or shine, weekend or weekday, you're at your desk by seven. You're a workaholic, squared."

Somehow, Kane didn't mind being accused of that by his sister, it was hearing Beth suggest it that had bothered him.

"You still shouldn't just barge in—I might not have been alone," he suggested lamely.

"I'm sure the reporters are going to report that next." With a broad grin Shannon tossed her newspapers on the bed. "And they'll have a pretty good idea with whom."

"Sheeesh."

Kane picked up the first and saw a large picture of him talking with Beth on the bow of the ferry. He was leaning toward her, and they both seemed quite intent. The headline above the photo read,

Billionaire Hits It Off With Reluctant Date.

"That's not so bad," he muttered. "It was Sunday and must have been a low news day."

"Take a look at this morning's paper."

A low whistle came from Kane as he saw a neat sequence of pictures taken of him kissing Beth on the Victoria dock. The headline simply said,

WOWZA!!!

A sidebar article was titled,

Romance Blossoms In Victoria.

The first paragraph was devoted to speculation that Seattle's most eligible bachelor might be off the marriage market.

He sighed. "Beth is not going to like this."

His sister's face was mischievous, a clear signal she still had news to share…news that probably wouldn't make him sleep any better.

"Out with it," he ordered.

"There have also been numerous reports on the television, and Patrick's station has been flooded with callers, all wanting to know how it's going. He's got a major audience tuning in to hear the smallest development. So we thought that maybe you could keep seeing Beth for a while to keep the interest up. Patrick really hates asking for another favor, but you can't *buy* this kind of publicity."

Kane's gaze dropped back to the photos. They were relatively harmless, but they did suggest something was developing. Something intimate.

And they were also an excuse to go see Beth.

Damn. He'd sworn he would never do Patrick another favor. Of course, it was an oath he'd never be able to keep, but his resolve should have lasted a little longer.

"Get out," he told his sister. "And tell my assistant not to expect me today."

"She's going to have a heart attack."

"Shannon."

"I'm going, I'm going."

With a flip of her hand, Shannon sailed from the room. Kane waited until the front door clicked behind her, then climbed from his bed. Fifteen minutes later he was in his Mercedes, headed once more for Crockett, Washington.

Beth lay on her back and gazed at the cloudless sky as she swung back and forth. She'd watched the sun rise, and though the air was still cool in the shade, she

PLAY LUCKY 7 and get FREE Gifts!

HOW TO PLAY:

1. With a coin, carefully scratch off the gold area at the right. Then check the claim chart to see what we have for you — **2 FREE BOOKS** and a **FREE GIFT** — **ALL YOURS FREE!**

2. Send back the card and you'll receive two brand-new Silhouette Romance® novels. These books have a cover price of $3.99 each in the U.S. and $4.50 each in Canada, but they are yours to keep absolutely free.

3. There's no catch. You're under no obligation to buy anything. We charge nothing — **ZERO** — for your first shipment. And you don't have to make any minimum number of purchases — not even one!

4. The fact is, thousands of readers enjoy receiving books by mail from the Silhouette Reader Service®. They enjoy the convenience of home delivery...they like getting the best new novels at discount prices, BEFORE they're available in stores...and they love their *Heart to Heart* subscriber newsletter featuring author news, horoscopes, recipes, book reviews and much more!

5. We hope that after receiving your free books you'll want to remain a subscriber. But the choice is yours — to continue or cancel, any time at all! So why not take us up on our invitation, with no risk of any kind. You'll be glad you did!

We can't tell you what it is...but we're sure you'll like it! A surprise **FREE GIFT** just for playing LUCKY 7!

NO COST! NO OBLIGATION TO BUY!

NO PURCHASE NECESSARY!

**Scratch off the gold area with a coin.
Then check below to
see the gifts you get!**

YES! I have scratched off the gold area. Please send me
the 2 Free books and gift for which I qualify. I understand I am
under no obligation to purchase any books as explained on the
back and on the opposite page.

315 SDL DNKQ   215 SDL DNKK

FIRST NAME   LAST NAME

ADDRESS

APT.#   CITY

STATE/PROV.   ZIP/POSTAL CODE   (S-R-05/02)

Worth **2 FREE BOOKS** plus a **FREE GIFT!**

Worth **2 FREE BOOKS!**

Worth **1 FREE BOOK!**

Try Again!

The Silhouette Reader Service® — Here's how it works:

Accepting your 2 free books and gift places you under no obligation to buy anything. You may keep the books and gift and return the shipping statement marked "cancel." If you do not cancel, about a month later we'll send you 6 additional books and bill you just $3.15 each in the U.S., or $3.50 each in Canada, plus 25¢ shipping & handling per book and applicable taxes if any.* That's the complete price and — compared to cover prices of $3.99 each in the U.S. and $4.50 each in Canada — it's quite a bargain! You may cancel at any time, but if you choose to continue, every month we'll send you 6 more books, which you may either purchase at the discount price or return to us and cancel your subscription.

*Terms and prices subject to change without notice. Sales tax applicable in N.Y. Canadian residents will be charged applicable provincial taxes and GST.

If offer card is missing write to: Silhouette Reader Service, 3010 Walden Ave., P.O. Box 1867, Buffalo NY 14240-1867

BUSINESS REPLY MAIL
FIRST-CLASS MAIL   PERMIT NO. 717-003   BUFFALO, NY

POSTAGE WILL BE PAID BY ADDRESSEE

SILHOUETTE READER SERVICE
3010 WALDEN AVE
PO BOX 1867
BUFFALO NY 14240-9952

NO POSTAGE
NECESSARY
IF MAILED
IN THE
UNITED STATES

could tell it would be a warm afternoon. Her leg was slung over the edge of the double-wide hammock, nudging the ground every so often to keep the movement going.

She shouldn't have gotten so upset with Kane and being kissed, but she'd never felt anything like that before.

Kane O'Rourke was practically a stranger and yet her body had gone off like a firecracker in July. Cripes, if she'd been like that with Curt it would have been nearly impossible to wait for the wedding before going to bed together. Beth moved restlessly and she wished she had a big old cat curled up next to her. Hammocks and purring cats should go together.

"Oh…blast," she muttered, a strong kick of her foot sending the hammock in a wide arc.

She'd had a lot of ideas about sexual attraction and her own body—wrong ideas, apparently. Kane had shattered every one of her preconceptions on those subjects.

In the back of her mind she registered the sound of a gate opening and closing, but she was too deep in thought to pay attention.

"Nice yard you have back here," said a deep voice.

Kane.

It didn't surprise her, though he was the last person she should have expected. As usual, he looked sophisticated and sexy, even in his jeans and shirt. A far cry from her worn shorts and sweatshirt with the sleeves whacked off above the elbow. She was dressed for messy work; in a couple hours she was going to a painting party down at the family crisis center.

"To what do I owe the honor?" Beth asked. "Weren't you supposed to go back to work today?"

Kane shrugged and slid into the hammock, with his head down by her feet. He tucked a couple of newspapers between them and yawned lazily. Her heart turned over. As an overworked businessman he was attractive; relaxing in a hammock he was devastating.

"Kane?"

"I take it you haven't read the paper." He said it more as a statement, than a question, and Beth stuck her head up.

"Am I not going to like what I read in the newspaper?" she enunciated carefully.

"Well, that depends on how good a sense of humor you have," he drawled. "Take a look and see for yourself."

Her pulse skipping, Beth grabbed the newspapers he'd brought and scanned them quickly. It didn't look that bad, certainly no worse than she'd expected *before* the weekend started. After all, she'd gone on a "date" with one of the richest, most handsome men in America. There were bound to be stories and questions and people wondering if it would lead to anything.

"Could have been worse," she said.

"Lots," Kane agreed.

"So why are you here?"

For the first time since they'd met, he seemed at a loss for words, and Beth's eyes narrowed suspiciously.

"*Kane?*"

"Uh, well, it seems my brother's radio station is getting flooded with calls. I guess the suggestion of a romance between us is stirring up a storm of interest. Shannon says it's all over the television, too."

Beth levered herself up on her elbows, instantly alarmed. "They don't know about the…the park?"

"No."

He shook his head and she sank back relieved.

"Not so far as I know," he added.

"Oh, great. Not so far as you know. That's really reassuring." She pushed the newspapers at Kane and covered her eyes with her arm. "Do you think *Hard Copy* will notify you before they run the story, or do we have to hold our breath until then?"

"I could have Shannon check it out, but then I'd have to explain what happened, and I thought you probably wouldn't want me to."

Beth shuddered. No, she didn't want his sister knowing about the park. "Let's keep it between us," she said. "And hope it *stays* between us."

Kane was silent for a long minute and Beth opened her eyes.

"Well?"

"I wanted to explain," he said slowly. "About that night."

"I don't think I can handle any more explanations."

A long sigh came from his chest. "But you need to understand. When I called it a mistake, it was because I've lived with prying reporters and cameras for a long time and knew better than to take that kind of chance. But you don't have any reason to think about dodging gossip on some entertainment news program."

Kane watched Beth's expression and knew she didn't entirely believe him. Why should she? He'd handled things badly, hurting her feelings along with her pride.

"Well, anyway…everyone is awfully interested in our so-called romance, and they're listening to Patrick's radio station in droves because his DJ's are…uh…"

"Talking about it?"

"Yeah. I listened to KLMS on the drive over—apparently they've started an hourly marriage report update. Will we say 'I do,' or won't we. That sort of thing," he said, disgusted.

Beth glared. "I'm sorry it's so awful. They must think you've lost your mind to be interested in someone like me."

Jeez.

When it came to Beth he was an expert at sticking his foot in his mouth. "Actually I figure everyone is amazed at my improved taste in women, but I don't enjoy being in the headlines. I've avoided the media spotlight as much as possible, and now we're both in the middle of it."

She didn't look annoyed, just thoughtful, and he drew a breath of relief.

"As much as I hate it, this kind of interest could go a long way toward making Patrick's station a success. So he thought it might help if the two of us were seen together a few more times. And since we're going to be in the public eye whether we want to be or not, it seems harmless."

"A fake romance for publicity's sake?"

"Not just for that," Kane said quietly.

He drew another deep breath of fresh air and glanced around Beth's backyard. Her house was small, but it was located on a large plot of land, bound at the far end by a wooded area. Flowers grew in cheerful profusion around a rock garden, and water trickled from a fountain in the center of a lily pond. On the opposite side he spotted a plentiful vegetable garden.

Like Beth, it was calm and peaceful, with a beautifully understated complexity. This was a garden that she'd taken time to design and grow and appreciate.

"There's nothing fake about wanting to become friends," Kane said simply. "I like being with you. I feel different, better, more the way I used to before things got so complicated. You're good for me."

"I don't see how that can be true."

"It is." He stretched lazily and thought about the mountain of work on his desk. He had a large staff, maybe it was time to start delegating. Things wouldn't always be done the way he liked, but that wasn't necessarily bad. Not if he could lie on a hammock and enjoy a summer day with a friend.

Of course, he'd never wanted to make love to a friend the way he wanted to make love to Beth. *That* was a wrinkle he'd have to learn to handle.

"How about it, Beth? Surely you can stand spending some time with me. We were enjoying ourselves before I went and blew it."

Beth rolled on her side, with her back to Kane to keep him from seeing things she didn't want him to see. She didn't have any illusions. While he seemed to have a fleeting attraction to her, nothing would come of it, not even friendship.

The hammock dipped for an instant as he twisted, then Beth felt a blade of grass tickling her bare instep.

"Stop that," she ordered, curling her foot.

"Only if you'll tell me what you're thinking."

"I'm thinking I'll look ridiculous."

"That would be me. Everyone is going to roll their eyes and say I'm lusting after a sweet thing young enough to be my daughter."

She turned around with an exasperated frown. "I'm twenty-six, not sixteen. Unless you got a much earlier start in the romance department than most boys, you're nowhere near old enough to be my father."

He chuckled. "There's an eleven year difference in our ages. That's quite a bit."

"No, it isn't."

"Yes, it is. I'll be called everything from a cradle robber to baby snatcher."

"Then why bother?"

Kane's shoulders lifted and dropped. "I have trouble saying no to my family. Though in this case I was looking for an excuse to call you. I didn't like the way we left things yesterday."

"We didn't leave it any 'way.'"

His eyes grew more serious. "That's what I mean. You were hurt and angry—with good reason—and I couldn't help it. I'm used to being able to fix things."

Drat. Beth sighed and rested her cheek in the palm of her hand. She didn't know what to do. This was Kane's chance to help his stubbornly independent brother, and she could help. She believed in families, which is why the Crockett Family Crisis Center was so important to her.

On the other hand, since meeting Kane, her safe, comfortable life had become inadequate. Of all the men in the world, why did it have to be Kane O'Rourke to upset everything?

"All right," Beth agreed reluctantly. "But I'm due at a painting party down at the crisis center in a little over an hour, so I can't talk about it now."

"Sounds like a good start to me. Would they mind if you brought someone along?"

She stared.

An image of Kane O'Rourke patching drywall and getting splattered with flat latex didn't add up.

"Uh, you understand I'm talking about paint," she said. "The kind that comes in gallon-size cans and gets slapped on walls and windowsills? This isn't an art gala with wine and cheese tasting.''

"I figured that—Crockett is nice, but it isn't an art gala sort of town. It's all right if I go, isn't it?''

"Er…yeah, the more the merrier. We're all volunteers. And a reporter is coming to do a story, so I guess the publicity would help the stuff with your brother. As a matter of fact, that will probably be enough. Only it doesn't seem like your kind of thing—it's messy and a lot of physical work.''

He bristled the way he usually did when she suggested he wasn't like regular people. "Trust me, it's my thing. But I don't understand why you aren't having the place professionally painted with the money I donated.''

"It wasn't supposed to look like you'd paid me to go…'' Beth felt warmth creep into her face because that was exactly what he'd done. She continued hastily. "Which is why you postdated the check. I told the director about it this morning and he thinks it should be earmarked for staff positions. Besides, by getting people involved at this early stage, they might keep volunteering in the future.''

"Oh.'' Kane's brow creased thoughtfully. "That sounds sensible. How about going to lunch first? I didn't have breakfast and I'm starving.''

Still surprised, she nodded and rolled out of the hammock. "Sure. I'll get my shoes and meet you out front.''

Kane watched Beth walk toward the house and decided it was a good thing he hadn't been invited inside. Her tight, sweetheart bottom was outlined by her shorts in a way that made his fingers itch. And he was also having trouble keeping his mind off how nicely her breasts had fit into his hands.

"Have a little restraint," he mumbled, climbing to his feet.

He was almost sorry he'd suggested going to lunch. There was something seductive about swinging in a hammock all cuddled up with a sexy girl. Especially when he already knew how good that girl felt in his arms.

"Yeah, a *girl*," Kane reminded himself. Beth might not agree that eleven years was much of a difference, but it was.

He had too much experience, she didn't have any. She was a softhearted do-gooder, while he was just a hardheaded businessman with a talent for making money. Basically he was a cynic, and Beth was an idealist.

She deserved more than a burned-out workaholic.

Keep thinking that, son, and you might start to believe it.

The voice seemed to come from nowhere, but Kane knew better. It was his father's voice. For a while after his death Kane had heard him often—a memory of the elder man's wise counsel that replayed clear and true at crucial moments. It had gradually faded away, lost in the chaos of work and responsibility. Years had passed since Kane had heard it. Maybe the reason he was hearing it now was that Beth reminded him of better days.

His dad would have liked her.

I do, son. She'd make a fine wife.

"Whoa." Kane took a breath and shook his head.

Remembering the things his father had said was one thing, it was quite another to hear something more immediate. But he'd been working too hard. It was no wonder his imagination was working overtime.

Still, the voice was right. His father really *would* have liked Beth.

Nine hours later Beth watched Kane carefully clean one paint roller after another. He'd seemed uncomfortable at first with the informal group of volunteers, but then his charm had kicked in and everyone thought he was wonderful. It was just icing on the cake when he offered to buy pizza for dinner.

"Do you always throw money at a problem before you try anything else?" she asked curiously. They were alone, everyone else having broadly winked and said they needed some time together. The reporter had already departed, his trip having earned a bigger "story" than expected.

"Money talks," Kane said, sluicing water around the sink.

"Maybe, but community involvement is the only thing that gets a place like this going. We need volunteers and support and awareness, and no amount of money can make that happen. Sometimes it even gets in the way."

He opened his mouth as if to protest, then went back to his washing.

Sadness crept through Beth as she realized that Kane had gotten so used to being needed for his wealth, that he'd forgotten how to be needed for himself. Maybe that was the crux of the problem with his family. They wanted something besides his money, something he'd forgotten he was already giving them.

He was a good man, one of the best she'd ever known. The end of their brief acquaintance would be more difficult now that she knew him better. And it *would* end, she didn't have any doubt.

In the meantime…

Beth put her hand on Kane's arm. "They liked you before you bought them pizza," she said quietly. "It was nice, but not necessary."

"I don't know what you're talking about."

"Yes, you do."

Kane clenched his jaw, but when he looked at Beth the tension flowed away. Her eyes were filled with concern. She might not trust him. She might think he was just another rich guy, but she cared about his feelings.

Vaguely, in the back of his mind, he was getting the notion that money didn't always fix things. He'd been so determined to take care of his family after his father's death that he'd focused all his energy on making a fortune. That way, they'd never lose the security he wanted them to have. In the process he'd lost something of himself. He didn't know how to live anymore.

But Beth threw herself into everything with boundless enthusiasm…everything except love. If she ever let herself fall in love again it would be a heavenly gift for the lucky man.

"At least they're eating pizza, and letting us be alone," he murmured. "So some good came out of it. Besides, money *does* fix things. I've been able to make my mother comfortable."

"Mmm." Beth flicked her tongue over her lips and he groaned silently. "How often do you see her?"

"My mother? A couple times a month. More during the summer. There's a wildflower my father used to pick for her. Nobody else seems to get the right one, so I stop whenever I see them."

"You pick wildflowers for your mother?"

Kane shrugged. "It's nothing."

Beth smiled sweetly. "I'll bet those wildflowers mean more to her than any fancy appliance or furniture you've gotten for her. And you don't even know how special it is."

He rubbed a small fleck of paint from her chin. "They're just wildflowers, Beth. I pick them alongside the road."

"Jeez, you're so stubborn. Tell me, do you know her favorite color? And how about Shannon? What does she like?"

It was like a test and Kane couldn't see the importance of it. But he played along, because even if it didn't make sense, he liked the way he felt when Beth's eyes were warm and seemed to admire him.

"Mom's favorite color is periwinkle-blue. Shannon prefers green. She's big into classical music and anything French. She's also crazy about sweets with white chocolate and macadamia nuts. But I don't understand why you're asking. Those are little things."

A small, sad laugh came from Beth and she shook her head. "Sometimes the little things matter the most. Curt and I were going to be married, but he couldn't have told you my favorite color, or even what month I was born in. To be honest, I felt invisible when he was excited about something. He didn't mean to make me feel that way, but he did."

"You're not invisible, Beth."

"I know, and I know he loved me. But I used to wish he could remember some of those little things. You see, nobody ever has, and it would have been nice. That's all."

God...Kane felt the foundations of his world sway. How could anyone make Beth feel invisible? She would have been a precious child, and she was an even more extraordinary woman. Whether she accepted it or not, she had so much love to give the right man.

"I shouldn't tell you this, but I've hardly slept for the past two nights because of you," he murmured. "And that hasn't happened because of a woman since I was sixteen with uncontrolled hormones."

"I don't believe you were *ever* uncontrolled."

"You saw it Saturday night. Caution, good sense, all my father's words about how to treat a lady went flying out the window. Kissing you is as close to heaven as I've ever come."

Their gazes were locked as he lowered his mouth onto hers. It was sweet, so sweet, a temptation beyond words. Without a second thought he gathered her closer.

He shouldn't be doing it.

The only thing he had to offer was an affair, and Beth wasn't cut out for affairs. But it was so good, holding her, tasting the depths of her mouth. He was on the edge of losing control again when a light flashed brightly.

"What the…?"

"Great shot. Thanks," said the reporter they had met earlier, right before dashing out the door as if the hounds of hell were at his heels.

"Damn." Kane would have chased after him, but Beth caught his arm and shook her head.

"You'll just make it worse. Besides, that's probably all your brother needed—a great publicity shot. They'll be able to speculate about it for days."

"I didn't kiss you for publicity," Kane snapped. "I kissed you because you're a damned desirable woman and that's what I wanted to do."

"Oh."

Beth wasn't sure what to think. She didn't know how far Kane would go, or what he'd say, to take care of his family. They meant everything to him.

It was one of the reasons she admired him.

Chapter Seven

Kane walked into his executive assistant's office early the following morning and gave her a repressive look. She was a smart lady and a hard worker, but she didn't have any business grinning like that.

"So, I took a day off," he muttered defensively. "I've got a life, or didn't you know it?"

"That'll be a surprise to everyone in the Western Hemisphere."

He gave her a fierce look, then spoiled it by grinning himself. "Okay, let's say my priorities have been a little off. I'm checking into an attitude readjustment clinic today."

"Sure, you are."

Libby's open disbelief didn't bother him. He'd heard so many pointed comments about his lack of a life that most of it just rolled off like water from a duck's back...all except the things Beth said. Why he cared what a skinny little innocent from Crockett had to say, he didn't know. He *did* know that skinny little innocent had the ability to make him hotter than he ever remembered feeling in his life.

Actually there was nothing skinny about the way Beth fit into his arms. Her breasts had satisfied him more than all the overblown women he'd ever dated, and she was smart, kind, funny and a damned good kisser.

But still an innocent. And still too young.

A sigh came from Kane's chest that seemed dredged from the bottom of his soul. He couldn't marry her; she deserved a full-time husband. He couldn't have an affair with her; once upon a time his dad would have taken a stick to him for even thinking about it. There were certain rules of behavior for real men, and it had nothing to do with what he did or didn't eat.

So if marriage and an affair were impossible, that left friendship. He just had to convince his body to accept friendship. Problem was, his body kept remembering kisses in the dark, and his ears kept hearing the eager little sounds Beth made when he caressed her slim body.

Jeez.

"By the way," Kane said, walking toward his adjoining office door. "I'm leaving in an hour. I want you to clear my schedule for the next two weeks. I'm taking some more time off."

Libby's mouth formed the words *oh my God,* but she seemed temporarily robbed of speech.

"Got that?" he asked. It was nice to make at least one woman speechless. He'd certainly never managed with his sisters or mother. The O'Rourke women were a hardy lot with angelic smiles and short-fuse tempers. In that respect, Beth was just like his family.

His assistant nodded shakily, reminding him of a

bobble-head doll. "What should we do about...uh, anything that comes up?"

Kane only had to think for a fraction of a second. If he was going to get a real life, he'd have to let go of a few things. "Neil can handle it. He's been aching to take over. Let him."

Neil was one of Kane's younger brothers—a Harvard graduate with nerves of steel when it came to delicate business negotiations. He'd worked on mergers in both Japan and Germany, so he was familiar with both the domestic and international aspects of the business.

"I'll draft a letter of authorization for your signature," Libby said, back to her old efficient self.

"Fine. He can use my office while I'm gone, unless you have a problem with that...?"

Her eyes flickered slightly. "No. Of course not."

Kane hesitated at the door. Libby and Neil had gone out on a single date after she'd first started with the company, which apparently had turned into a disaster of megaproportions. Since then their relationship could only be described as hostile.

"Are you certain it's all right?" Kane asked quietly. In many ways he thought of Libby as another sister, but she was also a valued employee and he wouldn't upset her for the world.

She plastered a professional smile in place and nodded. "You worry too much, boss. Enjoy your time off."

Kane thought about Beth's peaceful home and backyard, about hammocks and paint parties, and smiled. Who could have imagined that slapping paint on walls and eating stale doughnuts would be so much fun? Or that he'd skip work to do more of the same?

God, Beth made him feel good. It had been ages since he'd slept so well. Some of it was doing something for the community, but mostly it was working side by side with her. He *was* uncomfortable about pretending to pursue a romance for the publicity but his brother needed him...and the way Beth made him feel was irresistible.

"I'll enjoy it. You can be sure about that, Libby. Very sure."

Beth leaned back in the shower and let cool water pour over her. For a woman who liked nothing better than sleeping late *and* who had a few days vacation, she'd been getting up awful early. Actually it was more a matter of not being able to sleep, than waking up with the sunrise.

"Why did I let him kiss me again?" she muttered, sticking her nose into the stream of water.

She'd been working in the garden and was hot, sweaty and cranky, and it was only nine in the morning. If that wasn't bad enough, she'd taken a look at the newspaper when it was delivered. The local paper was having a field day with the latest picture, and the city newspapers would probably pick it up as well. There was nothing personal about their curiosity. The only reason they were interested in her was that they thought Kane O'Rourke was interested.

"Yeah, right," Beth said, and felt like crying.

Kane might have a fleeting physical response to her, but it wouldn't last. She probably wouldn't even see him again.

Beth thumped her forehead on the cool tile wall. "Why did I kiss him?" she moaned. "I'm an idiot."

Beneath Kane's expensive, conservative suits was

another man altogether, a man that made her heart yearn for something she'd lost once already. Which was ridiculous. Kane was a nice man and she liked him, nothing more. *You were lucky to find love once,* a voice reminded her, *it couldn't happen again.*

The doorbell rang as she stepped from the shower and she wrapped a robe around her. Her business partner usually stopped by this time in the morning, so she hurried to the door and threw it open, only to yelp and scurry backward.

"Yikes."

Kane grinned and held up two white paper sacks. "Coffee and apricot Danish. I thought we'd discuss our next move."

Beth gathered the lapels of the robe closer to her throat and glared. "What move?"

"Our pretend romance."

"Wasn't last night enough?"

His gaze wandered down the silk robe clinging to her skin, lingering at small swell of her breasts. Though he'd touched her intimately during their kiss in the park and she didn't have any reason for embarrassment, heat gathered in her cheeks.

"What was that?" he murmured.

She stomped her foot down for emphasis. "I asked if last night wasn't enough. Have you *seen* the local newspaper?"

"Nope."

"Well, take a look." Beth hurried into the kitchen where she'd left the paper and spun around with it in her hand, only to bump into him.

He caught her arms to prevent her from falling, smiling wider as her robe opened. She shoved the paper in his face and covered herself again.

Lordy, the man was impossible. To be honest, she wasn't terribly upset about the headline *or* the picture. Not that she enjoyed the notoriety, but she'd expected something like it when she agreed to a pretend romance. The whole thing would die down the next time Kane squired a woman to the opera or a symphony, or wherever he usually took his dates.

The thought was depressing, so Beth pushed a wet piece of hair from her forehead and watched as Kane read the newspaper.

"Isn't that terrible?" she asked.

"It's not so bad," he said.

"Billionaire Woos Local Beauty?" Beth said, rolling her eyes. "That's what I call wild hyperbole."

"Not really. I *am* a billionaire."

"But I'm not beautiful," she retorted.

"I think you are."

She twirled her finger in the international gesture that signaled he was crazy. "Then your vision needs to be checked."

"My vision is perfect."

Kane folded the paper and set it on the table. He thought the headline was fine—a big improvement over *Wowza*—though he would have preferred their latest kiss remaining private. Kissing Beth had been something he wanted to do, not a publicity stunt.

As for being beautiful…her subtle beauty had hit him straight in the gut when she opened the door. It was hard to be sensible when she wore something so provocative, especially with the way damp silk clung, outlining the hard points of her nipples and the curves of her bottom.

He'd nearly had a heart attack at the sight.

"I…uh." He cleared his throat, struggling with his

self-control. "You should have better sense than to answer the door wearing a bathrobe."

Her shoulders lifted in a shrug and his gaze was
glued to the sensual glide of her body inside the silk.
"Normally I don't, but I was expecting my partner in
the store."

Something inside of Kane twisted and he tried to
remember if any of the recent newspaper articles had
said whether Beth's "partner" was a man or woman.
"Your partner?" he asked carefully. Jealousy was *not*
a pleasant sensation, nor was it something he knew
how to handle. He'd never been jealous before.

"Emily Carleton," Beth said, seeming not to notice
his tension. "She sold me a half interest in the business
after her daughter was born. I have the week off—
unless she goes into labor with her second baby—and
she comes over to talk before opening the store."

A woman.

Kane forced himself to relax. He didn't have any
right to be possessive, especially after reminding himself that he couldn't marry Beth or have an affair with
her. Really, he ought to have better sense.

"Uh...I left the coffee and Danish in the other room.
I'll get it."

He took several deep breaths before returning. This
confused rush of feelings *wasn't* what he'd planned for
the morning, but with Beth he never knew what was
going to happen. He'd avoided chance for so long, it
was a surprise to discover he liked unpredictability, at
least when it came to Beth Cox.

Back in the kitchen he found Beth rereading the paper with grim concentration. For Pete's sake, he'd
never known a woman more prickly about compliments. She might not be Miss Universe, but who said

Miss Universe was all that great? Besides, Beth had something even better then a huge bustline...she had a heart. And a soul that was perfectly lovely.

A woman like that deserved someone terrific, a man who could focus on her a hundred percent. Kane knew he wasn't that man, and no matter what she said, he wasn't convinced her dead fiancé had acted the way ordinary men acted. It might be her basic kindness making her exaggerate the other man's failings. Still, she had a wonderful gift for making him feel alive and special.

"Coffee?" he asked, pulling a cup from the bag. "I didn't know what you like, so I got latte and cappuccino."

She regarded him for a long minute, then sighed. "Cappuccino." Taking the cup, she sampled the contents and munched on a Danish. After a long minute she looked at him and sighed. "You aren't going away, are you?"

"Not if I can help it."

"But that article is going to get lots of publicity and listeners for your brother's radio station. We don't need to keep pretending."

"I'm not pretending about being friends—I'd really like it. So we'll have a few more dates, and let everyone believe it's a romance, when we really know we're becoming friends."

Beth blinked.

She was more confused than ever. Kane didn't have time for friendship with someone like her, any more than he was interested in a real romance. She had a mirror, she knew what she looked like. Besides he'd thoroughly explored her not-so-generous curves, so they weren't a mystery.

"It won't work," she said slowly. "I don't even know why everyone believes you could fall in love with me."

"Maybe the question everyone is asking is how could you fall in love with me," Kane suggested. "You're a terrific lady, while I'm just a guy with a lot of money."

He sounded so sincere that Beth stared. He didn't mean that, did he? But she was starting to wonder, he'd said so many things about his money being the only thing he had to give.

"Don't give me that, you're a wonderful man," she said, exasperated. "You're brilliant, you take care of your family, you're a great employer, you give to charity and pick wildflowers for your mother because they're the ones she likes. You might be old-fashioned when it comes to women, but it's kind of sweet, too, in an annoying way. On top of everything else, you're the handsomest man I've ever seen!"

Oh, God, did she really say that?

His smile grew. "Then why don't you want to be friends?"

"I didn't say that."

"So we can be friends, but romance is out," he said thoughtfully.

She screamed inside, wanting to shake and kiss him at the same time. Most of all, she was scared from the top of her head to the tips of her toes. Kane could tear her life apart again. He wouldn't do it deliberately, but it could happen just the same. The way he was making her feel was too frightening, too *wonderful*. She'd only end up hurting again.

"We can't even be friends," she said, trying to

sound reasonable. "Think about it. We live on different sides of Puget Sound—"

"That's what I thought, then I realized that's why they build roads and have car ferries."

"You're a wealthy man," she continued through gritted teeth. "While I own half of a clothing store—kid's clothes and maternity dresses. That kind of thing."

He nodded. "It's great, we're both businesspeople. It gives us extra stuff to talk about, though we've hardly run out of things to say."

Beth let out a muffled shriek. "You're not listening."

"Now, that isn't true. I'm hearing every word and simply explaining what you've missed."

"I haven't missed anything. I've never had a family, you've got gobs of family. You're a morning person, I hate morning."

He gave her a lazy, sensuous smile. "Bet I could make you love it."

Drat.

The suggestion made Beth lose her concentration, mostly because it was such a hot idea that she couldn't think about anything else for a minute. Not that she thought he was serious about teaching her to love morning, but the *way* he could teach her was an image too distracting to ignore.

Of course, he wasn't serious about any of it. He wanted to help his brother, and that was all. So how could she refuse? She might have never had a family, but that only made her appreciate them more.

"How about it, Beth?" Kane asked softly. "Let's spend some time together. Everyone else can think what they want. We'll just be ourselves."

That's what worried her. Kane O'Rourke was too much of everything. Temptation incarnate.

"Oh, all right. But no more kisses," she added hastily.

"I can't promise that."

"Why not?" she demanded.

Kane drew his finger down the inside line of her wrist. "Because I don't break promises, and that isn't one I can be sure of keeping. So, you go get dressed and we'll talk about what to do today."

"I was thinking about getting a kitten," she said without thinking.

"Great." Kane pulled out his cell phone. "I'll give my assistant a call. There must be some good cat breeders in the area. Did you have a particular breed in mind?"

Beth shook her head. "Yeah, a mutt cat."

An adorably confused expression crossed his face. "A mutt cat?" he repeated carefully. "I've never heard of it."

"You know, a Heinz 57 kitten. A little bit of everything. An *alley* cat who needs a home," Beth emphasized.

She didn't know how she'd decided to get herself a cat, maybe it was wanting a purring feline to cuddle up with her in the hammock, but the idea had burst out without any conscious plan. She loved animals and wasn't sure why she'd waited so long.

"Where do you get alley cats? I'm not taking you to some back street alley," Kane said, sounding appalled. "Wild cats can be dangerous. I'll trap one and get it tamed."

A giggle escaped Beth, though she tried to control it. "You really *do* live in a different world," she teased. "Kane, you adopt alley cats at the local animal shelter. The one in Crockett is a no-kill shelter and it's really nice."

"I suppose it's one of your charities."

"I've baked a few cakes for fund-raisers," she admitted. "They need a new building and it's expensive to keep a veterinarian on retainer. All the animals are tested for disease and get their shots and stuff."

Kane shook his head and fought the urge to hug Beth. She was the most tempting woman, with a heart so big it made him ache.

"All right," he agreed. "Get into some clothes, then let's go to the shelter and pick out your mutt cat."

She hesitated for an instant, then hurried out the door. Kane sipped his rapidly cooling latte, smiling at himself. Once upon a time he would have understood "mutt cat." When had he moved from adopting a needy pet at an animal shelter, to thinking only of expensive purebreds?

Beth was good for him in so many ways, though being friends wasn't sensible when he wanted her so much. Compared to Beth, other women lacked something—women with far more superficial beauty. Yet none of them had her radiant smile and sweet, giving, independently *stubborn* nature. Or the way she had of making him want to be a better man than he knew himself to be.

That was the kind of friend a man needed. He didn't have to have her for a lover.

Right?

He pondered the thought—and his reluctance to agree—all the way to the animal shelter. It was filled with dozens of cats and dogs with eager faces pressed against their cages.

Kane groaned when he saw Beth's eyes fill with tears at each enclosure. She obviously wanted to adopt them all. Though she'd said she wanted a kitten, she'd already picked out an enormous gray cat who hung in her arms and purred so loud it practically made the lightbulbs rattle. The tag on the cage had said his name was Smoke, and he'd been at the shelter for over a year, waiting for a home.

"I'll put the word out at my company," he said quickly. "Ask everyone to consider coming over to adopt a pet. I'll pay all the fees and everything. They can even come over on work time if they want. Whatever it takes."

"You will?" The hopeful look in her eyes turned him into mush. He would have offered the moon to make her feel better.

Just then a paw insinuated itself through the bars and snagged a clawful of Beth's hair.

"*Merooow!*" the kitten demanded. *I want to go home with you. Right now.*

Beth turned and smiled at the insistent scrap of fur and milk teeth. It was tiger-striped with long tufts of fur sticking up from its ears and between its toes.

"What do you think, Smoke?" she asked the cat cradled in her arms. "Can you deal with a little brother?"

The gray cat yawned and tucked its head inside her elbow. He was the mellow type. Food, a lot of love and a warm place to sleep were the requirements of his life.

Before Beth could be targeted by another feline con artist, Kane hustled her and the two cats into the lobby where he insisted on paying the adoption fees. The scrappy little kitten didn't appreciate going into the cardboard carrier or the car, but the adult settled into his box and promptly went to sleep. Insomnia plainly wasn't one of Smoke's problems.

The distress in Beth's expression grew with each siren scream of the kitten until she popped the carrier open and let it climb into her lap. Once freed, the animal settled down and proceeded to give himself a bath.

"You darling," she murmured, rubbing under his chin with her forefinger.

For the first time in his life, Kane envied a cat. Those two felines were going to be loved, petted and adored. They had it made. He cleared his throat. "I suppose you need food and litter and stuff?"

Beth winced. "That's right, I forgot. There's a vet's office down the street that probably carries supplies. If you don't mind stopping, I'll go in and get it."

He gave her a smile. "No problem, but I'll get what we need."

"Well...there's money in my purse, I'll get some out."

"It's just some cat food," he chided, swinging his legs from the car. "You just stay here and keep the kids out of trouble."

Keep the kids out of trouble.

Beth had trouble breathing at the ordinary way he'd said that. It was the danger of being around Kane, he was every woman's dream—tall, strong, sensitive, and so handsome that she wanted to tear his clothes off just for smiling. And she definitely had the urge to make a baby with him.

"Well, I don't need a baby. I have you, don't I?" she whispered to the spider-legged kitten cleaning his rump on her leg. It was an inelegant posture, but it helped rouse Beth's sense of humor. "You're a boudoir cat, right?"

Yawning, the kitten fell over on its side and went to sleep.

The sound of the trunk opening caught Beth's attention and she waited as Kane and one of the veterinary assistants made several trips in and out of the office. It seemed like an awful lot, so when Kane slid behind the steering wheel, she frowned.

"What did you get?"

"Just a few things you and the kids might need."

"*Kane,* you can't just buy—"

"*Beth,*" he said, mimicking her exasperated tone. "I can buy anything I want, and if I want to get some gifts for my new godchildren, I'm allowed."

"They aren't your...oh, pooh."

"How articulate." He tapped her nose and laughed. "I like being with you, Beth. There's never a dull moment when we're together."

It seemed to her it must be awfully dull for a man like Kane. She'd dragged him to work at the crisis center where he'd slapped paint on walls for nine long hours. Now he'd seen the glamorous interior of an animal shelter and vet's office. Sure, the excitement never ended in Crockett.

Not that *she* thought it was dull, but she couldn't see Kane enjoying such ordinary things. She liked her life, or at least she had before he'd come around and upset everything. Actually she *still* liked her life, but now there was a nagging sense of something missing. The worrisome part was wondering how she'd feel after things settled down and she was in Crockett, while Kane returned to his world in Seattle.

Back at the house she was even more put out when

she saw that he'd gotten everything from a mountain of gourmet food to cat beds, toys, flea products and two electric "self-cleaning" litter boxes.

"They said these things are great," Kane murmured when she protested. He was sitting on the floor, reading the instructions. Before long he had them both assembled and filled with litter. "Where do you want them? You'll need a place with an outlet."

Beth shook her head in disgust and directed him to the spare bedroom. It would keep the smell from the kitchen and her own bedroom, and give the cats some privacy while doing their business.

Never, in her wildest dreams, could she have imagined Kane O'Rourke putting a litter box together. He'd seen something that needed doing, and had done it. No fuss or protestations, or even an expression of distaste for something beneath him. It was strange. For a man with a lot of money, he didn't mind getting his hands dirty.

But the strangest part of the whole day was when they all fell asleep on the hammock, with Smoke curled up on Kane's stomach and the kitten nestled in her hair.

Since there was nothing relaxing about Kane, Beth could only suppose it was due to them both being tired.

Chapter Eight

The next morning Beth's curiosity got the best of her and she tuned into the KLMS radio station. The first thing she heard was a drum roll and the dramatic announcement, *"O'Rourke Marriage Watch."*

She shook her head.

Did people honestly believe Kane would fall for someone like her? She was a nobody, and he was the most gorgeous man she'd ever seen. Most people didn't believe in fairy tales, and that's exactly what the radio station was trying to sell.

"Listen up, folks," said the disc jockey. "Things are looking hopeful for Kane O'Rourke ending his lonely bachelor existence. A little bird tells us that he and the charming Miss Cox picked out two cats at the Crockett Animal Shelter yesterday. While it isn't a station wagon, two kids and a dog, it's not a bad sign."

The DJ went on to extoll the animal shelter and its good work, an addition Beth was certain had come from Kane's prompting. He was a nice man and would be a perfect husband for the right woman. But she wasn't the right woman, and a pang went through Beth when she wondered how it would feel to hear he was getting married for real. And he would, eventually.

She'd never been a celebrity watcher. Famous people had never interested her. But it would be different with Kane; he'd kissed her, touched her, laughed and teased and made her feel just a little bit beautiful.

A springy ball of fluff leaped onto the windowsill and stared out at a crow, preening his blue-black feathers in the sunshine.

"Merroow."

Beth laughed and tugged the kitten's tail. She'd named him "Razzle" to match his dizzy personality.

"I don't think you're going to tackle him—he's twice your size. You need to stay inside unless I'm with you."

Razzle kept watching the crow and Beth looked at the clock for the tenth time in the past hour. She'd already worked in the garden, swept the entire house and taken a shower...all because Kane had said he'd "stop by" around ten. As a result she'd been awake since dawn, wondering if he'd really meant it.

"It doesn't matter if he didn't," she whispered.

It really didn't.

But all her protestations weren't worth a lick when the knock came on the door, making her pulse jump.

Kane smiled when she answered and held out a potted plant that Beth didn't immediately recognize. "I brought something for the kids. Do you think they'll like catnip?"

"They'll love it—almost as much as those jingle jangle balls you got them," she added dryly. "Did you know kittens never sleep at night? They don't even stand flat on their feet, they just dance around on the tips of their toes.''

''Sorry about that.''

''I'm the one who wanted a kitten.''

''So, you were.''

Kane thought he could get lost in the rueful laughter in Beth's eyes. He was getting in deeper than he'd expected, involving himself in the everyday doings of her life and loving every minute.

He cleared his throat. ''You mentioned being a baseball fan, so I'm getting a private suite at the Mariners' game on Sunday. That is, if you don't have anything planned for the weekend.''

''A private suite?'' Her nose wrinkled. ''Don't do that. I'm sure tickets are available in the upper deck, and there's no such thing as a bad seat at Safeco Field.''

''But wouldn't you rather go in style and miss the peanut shells and spilled soda?''

''I'd rather feel like I'm at the ballpark—peanut shells and everything—instead of being stuck in a room with a window.''

''It isn't like that.''

''Close enough.'' She softened her remark with a smile and carried the catnip to the kitchen.

Kane followed, shaking his head. There weren't many women like Beth. The rest of his family was dying to meet her—they loved anyone willing to sass him, and Shannon had told them about the morning Beth had stormed into his office.

''By the way,'' he said. ''Sunday evening is O'Rourke family night. My mother wants us to come over after the game and have dinner with everyone.''

To his surprise, Beth looked alarmed. "She doesn't think we're really involved."

"No," he assured quickly. "I'd never let Mom get her hopes up for nothing. She's pretty anxious for more grandchildren—she only has my youngest sister's girls to spoil."

Her face still worried, Beth spun around and turned on the water at the sink.

A deep groan came from the plumbing a split second before a jet of water shot toward the ceiling. She yelped and stumbled backward, staring at the faucet handle that had come off in her fingers.

"Oh...drat," she muttered.

"Drat? Is that all you can..." Kane rolled his eyes and strode across the kitchen. "Grab a pot and direct that water into the sink while I shut it off."

"That's all right." Beth dropped the broken handle and swatted wet hair from her face. "You don't have to do anything. I can manage."

He just grunted, dropped to the floor and opened the cupboard under the sink.

Beth glared, but grabbed her largest soup pot and pushed it over the fountain rising from her sink. She was drenched already, and Kane soon would be. Men could be so impossible. They thought they knew it all and could fix anything in the world.

Kane muttered to himself as he shifted cleaning supplies and the garbage pail out of the way.

"Really, I can take care of this," Beth insisted. She hadn't quite been able to contain the water with her pan and sprays still shot out of the sink, over both of them, along with the floor. At least the ceiling was being spared.

If not her sanity.

She looked down and saw Kane's shirt pull across his broad shoulders, the drenched fabric clung, displaying a nice set of muscles. Not to mention the sight of his killer buns, framed by wet denim. Sensations, hot and uncontrolled, spun through her body and she groaned.

"Really, I can take care of it," she said, trying not to sound desperate, even if that's the way she felt.

"I don't walk out on women needing my help," he growled from the bowels of the cupboard.

"Don't lay this on me being a woman. I don't need your help." It wasn't strictly true—not at the moment—but that wasn't the point. Besides, if the sink had broken when she was alone, she would have handled everything. Sometimes you didn't have a choice except to take care of things.

And it was easier taking care of things without a man around who made you feel such confusing emotions.

"Damn, these knobs don't want to move. When was the last time you turned the water off down here?"

"Never. There hasn't been any need."

"How long have you lived in this house?"

"Over four years." For a moment Beth's mind drifted back to the day when she'd decided she had to go on living, even though Curt was gone. She'd impulsively made an offer on the house and had moved in within the month.

"Oh, good," Kane said, his voice muffled. "This one is turning a little."

The pressure lessened, then slowly became a trickle, before stopping completely. Beth cautiously let go of the pan, then shook her head to dislodge a drop of water clinging to her chin. She glanced down again as

Kane edged his way out of the cupboard, thoroughly doused by her kamikaze plumbing.

"I'm sorry," she said. "I don't suppose you brought a change of clothing?"

"I don't suppose I did," he returned affably. "Let's get some of this water cleaned up."

They swilled water from the floor with her mop and a pile of bath towels. She was throwing a load of her formerly clean towels into the washing machine when she heard some electronic beeps and turned around to see Kane press a button on his cell phone, then put it to his ear.

"O'Rourke here. Get Miles on the phone," he ordered. "Miles? This is Kane. I want you to get one of our facilities maintenance men over to 551 Jacobson South."

Beth instantly waved her hand to get his attention and shook her head. "No."

He was obviously not listening. "I want the best man with plumbing. Make sure he brings the correct fixtures and pipes to repair a kitchen sink." Kane looked into her old sink and frowned. "And a new sink."

"Now, wait just a minute," Beth exploded. "You aren't doing any such thing."

Kane hunched his shoulder away, more intent on his conversation with "Miles" than hearing her objections.

"Yeah," he said into the phone. "The entire unit needs to be replaced, including the shutoff valves. Someone else can bring the sink to speed things up." He was silent for a moment. "I don't know, just a new double sink—something a woman would like. A good one."

Beth put her hands on her hips and glared. She

wasn't big enough to take the phone away from him, so she'd just have to wait until he disconnected...and let him have it.

"Yes, I'll meet him here." Kane pushed another button on his phone and dropped it onto the table, which was probably the only truly dry place in the kitchen.

"What do you think you're doing?" she demanded.

He unbuttoned the cuffs of his shirt and rolled the sleeves up his arm. "Getting a plumber to help. We have a maintenance staff at the Crockett Mill."

"Absolutely not. Call and tell them not to come."

He looked at her in astonishment. "I'll do no such thing, Beth. Your plumbing must date back to the Depression. It has to be repaired. I can do part of the work, but I'm no expert and it needs to be done right."

Beth let out a long-suffering, patient sigh. "I know it's old, and I'll take care of it. I can handle my own problems."

"Of course you can, but I can get someone here faster. It takes forever to get a plumber for this kind of work. Believe me, I know."

She tapped her fingers on her thighs and gave him a narrow look. "Reality check, Kane. Most of us *non*-billionaire types manage to get through the catastrophes of life fairly well. We even manage to survive without running water in our kitchens for a day or two. I'm doing the repairs myself."

"Do you have experience running pipes under the house and replacing cast-iron porcelain sinks?" he asked. "Those things weigh almost two hundred pounds. You talk tough, but there's no way you can lift one by yourself."

"Maybe not." She pushed her damp hair back in exasperation. "But I'm not replacing the sink or any of that other stuff. I'll just get a book on fixing the doohickey thing that broke.''

"The doohick..." Kane's eyes widened. "Honey, *everything* needs to be replaced, it's falling apart."

"You aren't listening," Beth practically shrieked. She drew a calming breath. "Ordinary people do things on a budget. And if that means fixing just one part of the sink at a time, then so be it."

"But you—"

The doorbell rang, cutting him off. "If that's your plumber," she said over her shoulder. "He can just leave."

Kane shook his head, unable to understand why women were so contrary. And Beth in particular. Big deal. So he'd asked one of his employees to come over and work on her kitchen. He did the same thing for his mother and sisters when the occasion arose, and they didn't object.

The exaggeration made him sigh.

Okay, so they *did* object, but he didn't understand his family's protests, any more than he understood why Beth minded so much. There was a problem, so he was taking care of it. And it wasn't as if he was giving her a diamond necklace, it was just some plumbing. Nothing special about a damn sink.

"Hi, Nick," he heard Beth say in the other room. "Mmm, look at Katie, sound asleep. She's such an angel."

"Just like her mother," a deep voice rumbled.

Katie?

Kane poked his head into the living room and saw a man standing inside the front door, holding a golden-haired child asleep on his shoulder. Obviously this wasn't the plumber.

"You're soaking wet, what happened?" the man asked.

"Slight disaster with the kitchen sink. But I think we've saved the house from floating off the foundation."

"We?"

"Uh…yeah. I've got company." She sounded embarrassed and uneasy and Kane wondered if this "Nick" would assume more was going on with her "company" than plumbing repairs.

"Hello," Kane said, once again bitten by jealousy. He stepped inside the room and crossed his arms over his chest.

Perhaps it was just the surge of adrenaline he'd gotten from dealing with the broken water pipe, but he wanted to boot the other man out of Beth's house and tell him never to come back. Especially with the way she looked right now, the coolness of her wet shirt turning her nipples into tight knots. It didn't matter that Nick didn't seem the least bit interested in her chest.

Beth shifted from one foot to the other. "Nick Carleton, this is Kane O'Rourke."

Nick nodded. "Do you need some help?" he asked. "I've got my tools in the Blazer."

Beth smiled. "That would be great, if you're not too—"

"We don't need any help," Kane said, cutting her off.

She planted her hands on her hips again and gave him a fierce look. "Kane."

"Beth," he mimicked right back. "Why are you willing to accept Nick's help, and not mine?"

"Nick is a friend."

"And what am I?" he growled, annoyed. "I thought we settled that nonsense."

"I'm happy to help," Nick said hastily. "Besides, Beth takes care of Katie whenever we need, and she's my wife's business partner—and does more than her fair share, too. Especially with Emily being pregnant."

Distracted, Beth looked back at Nick. "How *is* Emily? She said she was having Braxton-Hicks contractions last night, but that I shouldn't come into the store unless she called."

Nick grinned so broadly that Kane knew, beyond a doubt, he was a one-woman man. Beth's relationship with Nick was that of a friend, nothing else.

"She's great," Nick said. "But I'm going crazy and the doctor says we're more than a week away. I kept hanging around the shop until she kicked me out—says I'm fussing too much."

"Don't forget I'm baby-sitting when the time comes."

"I won't forget." Nick glanced at Kane. "About the plumbing, I've done our entire house, so it's no big deal."

Kane shook his head. *He* wanted to be the one to take care of Beth's plumbing. His sisters would say he was just being stubborn and macho, but that's the way it was.

"I've got it under control."

Nick shrugged. "If that's what you want."

"You're both the limit," Beth snapped. "*I* have it under control, you just showed up at the wrong moment. Both of you can leave." She pointed to the door.

"Just like my wife. That's why they get along so well." Nick shared a commiserating smile with Kane and obeyed.

Kane didn't have any intention of following him.

"You, too," Beth said, tapping her foot.

"Nope. I don't have anything else to do, so I might as well keep busy with your sink."

Beth made a frustrated sound. "Men. You think you rule the universe."

Kane grinned. He loved that contrary expression of Beth's, which was a good thing since he saw it often enough. Her thick, long hair kept dripping water onto her shirt, keeping it damp. He was a crumb, but he also loved seeing that, as well. The pink, surprisingly large aureoles of her nipples were evident as they poked forward, pressing into the thin cotton shirt.

"Do you have something I could wear?" he asked huskily, needing to focus on something besides the things she did to him without half trying. "Some stretchy sweats, or something?"

Beth lifted her chin. "I don't care how stretchy they might be—if you fit into my clothing I'll shoot myself. Actually that isn't true, I'll shoot *you*."

The corners of his eyes crinkled into a smile. "Is that so?"

"Yes. But if you want to wrap up in a blanket, I can throw your stuff into the dryer."

"That's all right, I'll manage." Kane shook his head; he didn't want to be clutching a blanket around his naked self when one of his employees arrived. Almost as if in summons to his thought, he saw a truck pull into Beth's driveway with the O'Rourke Industries logo on the side.

"Help has arrived," he murmured.

Beth's gaze narrowed. "You can just tell 'help' to leave."

"Nope." He straightened and glanced around the

room; it was neat and clean—no carelessly discarded clothing to cover Beth's chest. "But you need to change," he said.

"Why?" she asked. "I'm no wetter than you are."

"It doesn't matter as much for me." He motioned to her T-shirt.

Beth looked down and gasped. Of all days, why couldn't she have worn a bra this morning? She didn't really need one, but it would have concealed more.

"Don't worry," he murmured. "I'm enjoying the show, and Nick is probably so besotted with his wife he wouldn't see a Playboy Bunny streaking naked through his bedroom."

"I don't have anything to show," she growled back.

"Hey, I like what I see." His voice deepened, along with the color in his eyes. "And it reminds me of how good you feel." He reached out and brushed the back of his hand over a jutting nipple. "We could always tell the plumber to leave and spend the rest of the day…remembering."

Beth's heart jammed itself into her throat.

With his other hand he cupped the back of her neck and drew her closer. The warmth of his body was undefeated by their drenching and it penetrated the chill surrounding her. She even felt it advancing on the protective wall around her heart.

No. She couldn't feel that way again, couldn't take the pain when it fell apart. Yet something about Kane was so seductive…the gentleness in his touch, the understanding in his blue eyes. The expression that said he'd been through it, too, the pain and loss, and that he knew how hard it was to trust in life again.

He tugged ever so carefully on her sensitive nipple and heat streaked through her veins. She opened her mouth, but her moan was lost between his lips as they pressed down.

It wasn't fair.

A man shouldn't have so much power. He shouldn't be able to seduce a woman with laughter and tender looks.

He shouldn't be able to seduce her at all.

The sound of a truck door slamming and a loud clanking intruded, shattering the moment. Beth reluctantly drew back, her body less anxious than her heart and mind to abandon the warmth Kane offered.

"Get something dry on," Kane muttered, his voice barely recognizable. He looked every bit as stunned as she felt. But that couldn't be true.

The doorbell rang and she stumbled to her bedroom, leaving him to answer the door. At the moment independence didn't seem as important as regaining her sanity.

She'd been tempted, *oh* so tempted.

By the time she'd changed into dry clothing, the two men were in the kitchen, deep in discussion about the antiquated state of her plumbing. "You're right, it needs the full job," the other man agreed.

"I'm taking care of it myself," she announced, her independence reasserting itself.

"She's being difficult," Kane complained. But a smile played on his mouth and he winked at the other man.

Beth wanted to kick him—he was enjoying himself entirely too much. Worse, he'd recovered his equilibrium far too quickly, acting as if they'd never kissed at all. Men were rats.

"I am not being difficult," she said.

He cocked his head. "See what I mean? She has this stubborn idea about not accepting anyone's help."

"I accepted Nick's offer to help, then you sent him away." Beth's glare should have sizzled Kane to his toes, but he figured having four sisters had made him immune.

The plumber smiled kindly. "I'm happy to help. You probably don't remember, but your fiancé, Curtis Martin, he saved my sister's husband from a house fire a few years back. So you can take me off the clock, Mr. O'Rourke—this is on the house."

"I...that's nice of you, but it isn't necessary," Beth said.

The peculiar expression in her face made Kane's stomach twist. "Let's talk," he said, catching her arm and pulling her into the backyard.

"What is it?"

Awkwardly he stroked his hands down her arms. He wanted to comfort her, and he wanted her to forget she'd ever been in love with another man. Funny, he'd never been the possessive type before, and Beth wasn't even close to being his, no matter what his gut instincts told him.

"I'm no hero, Beth, but I can help fix some pipes. And we *are* friends, even if you don't want it that way."

She let out a breath and focused on him. "A hero? What's that supposed to mean?"

"Like..." He hesitated. "Like your fiancé, that's what you were thinking about, wasn't it?"

Beth shook herself and looked—really *looked*—at Kane. He didn't understand, but she didn't expect him to. She'd loved Curt, but in a way he'd been a selfish boy, more concerned with doing what he wanted than sharing his life with her. In time he would have learned to put aside his whims and become a responsible family man, but she couldn't see him doing what Kane O'Rourke had done. He wouldn't have given up his own dreams to support his mother and siblings. At the very least he would have resented it.

Looking in from the outside, Kane had a glamorous life, but it was really just hard work and doing the right thing. Heroes came in different styles, and she rather liked the hero standing in front of her.

"Don't ever think you come up short, Kane O'Rourke," she said quietly. "Some things take more courage than risking your life, and I don't think you'd ever hesitate to do what was necessary."

"I'm not exactly deprived, Beth."

She sighed, wishing she could hug him. But he might not understand and hugging led to other things. "Money isn't everything. You wanted to be an engineer, didn't you? But you quit school and worked after your father died. And you do whatever it takes to help your family, even at the expense of your business."

"Well...they're *family*," Kane said, clearly astonished that anyone would think of doing anything else.

"I know, and I hope they realize how lucky they are."

He lifted one eyebrow. "Actually they complain a lot—just like you."

Beth didn't laugh, because she understood more than Kane realized. "It's hard letting go, isn't it?" she said. "They used to need you a whole lot more, but now they're grown up and independent."

"They aren't that grown up."

She couldn't contain a giggle at his disgruntled tone. "Oh, Kane, you're going to be one of those old-fashioned protective fathers who doesn't want his daughter to date until she's thirty, or his son to have his own car until he's on Social Security.''

''Is that a proposal, Miss Cox?''

Beth grinned. ''Since you're all wet anyway, you might as well go fix my sink.''

''No comment, eh?''

''I think the news media has commented enough.''

With a smile, Kane ran his thumb over her lips, then sauntered back to the kitchen. He didn't know. Maybe heroes weren't easy to live with, and he felt awfully good when Beth said things like that.

Chapter Nine

It wasn't until Friday that Beth had a chance to think. Her plumbing nightmare hadn't scared Kane away as she'd expected, instead he'd come Thursday and spent the entire day.

They had planned to take the Carleton's boat out that morning, but Kane had gotten an emergency call from the office shortly after arriving. Before leaving he'd reminded her of their plans for the Sunday Mariners' game and dinner with his family, just in case he couldn't get back earlier.

"What do you think?" she murmured to Smoke, who was the coziest lap cat imaginable.

Smoke rolled so his tummy was exposed and purred loudly when she obliged by rubbing it. Razzle was off playing in the kitchen. She didn't let the cats go into the yard unless she was with them, and right now she didn't have the energy to chase after a twelve-week-old kitten with springs in his hind legs.

"I'm a putz," she mumbled to herself, slumping deeper into the living room couch.

Normally she loved being out in her garden, but without Kane it didn't interest her. And the hammock didn't have half its allure alone, though all they did was read and talk and sometimes go to sleep.

"I can't believe it," she whispered. "He *must* be bored." That had to be the answer, yet Kane gravitated toward the hammock every afternoon as if it was a magnet. Just thinking about the way he looked, lying there in his jeans and bare feet made her squirm with warmth.

A man's feet shouldn't be sexy.

They were just feet, for heaven's sake.

Smoke had fallen into a deep, boneless sleep when the doorbell rang. He opened one eye and complained when Beth slid him to the cushions.

"Sorry," she said, her heart illogically picking up speed.

It might be Kane. Maybe the emergency hadn't turned out to be so bad, and he'd decided there was time to come back to Crockett. Yet even as Beth formed the thought, she pushed it away and opened the door.

"Miss Cox, have you and Mr. O'Rourke had a fight?" asked a reporter, thrusting a microphone in front of her. "We understand he returned to Seattle less than an hour after getting here this morning."

"I...no, of course we haven't had a fight," Beth said, instinctively stepping backward from the onslaught of flashing cameras and questions.

"You've been spending a lot of time together. What happened?"

Her gaze narrowed. "Two of his employees were

critically injured in a traffic accident,'' she said crisply. ''He went back to Seattle to meet with the families and see if he could help.''

They ignored her obvious displeasure, being more interested in a supposed romance, than the truth.

''Has he proposed?''

''When are you getting married?''

A dozen other questions came pouring out, with no one waiting for a response, and Beth took tighter hold of the door. She wanted to help Kane's family, but she couldn't lie for them.

''Kane and I are friends,'' she said. ''That's all.''

Knowing winks and disbelieving shakes of the head greeted her comment, along with some guffaws from the rear of the crowd. ''Mr. O'Rourke seems interested in more than friendship,'' called someone, waving one of the pictures of them kissing. ''How about this, Miss Cox?''

''It's personal,'' she muttered grimly. ''There's nothing more to say. I'm sorry you've wasted your time. Goodbye.''

She closed the door firmly and decided to disconnect her doorbell. The reporters had been bad enough after she'd first refused to go on the date, but she'd never expected so much hysteria over some kisses and dates.

A clunk from the kitchen sounded too loud to be caused by Razzle, so she hurried out and found a photographer taking pictures of the flowers on the table.

''What do you think you're doing?'' Beth demanded.

''Mr. O'Rourke brought you these, didn't he?''

Beth glared. ''You're trespassing on private property. Illegal entry is a crime in this state.'' She snatched the phone and dialed the police.

The photographer hastily disappeared out the open door and around the side of the house. The dispatcher answered and Beth explained what had happened; they promised to send out a squad car and warn the reporters to stay away or be arrested. Crockett was a nice town and took care of its own.

It made her feel better until she realized she hadn't seen Razzle for quite a while, and a sick feeling hit her when she remembered the door the photographer had left open.

She searched the house. No kitten. It was the same for the yard. She hunted the neighborhood, calling his name until her throat was raw.

Heartsick, Beth finally collapsed on the back step and tried to keep tears from escaping. She'd fallen in love with the funny little kitten, and now he was gone. It was some comfort to think he might return when he got hungry, but there weren't any guarantees. It was a big world.

And she didn't have much luck keeping the things she loved.

The phone rang, and kept ringing on and off until she dragged herself inside.

"Yes?"

"Beth? Is everything all right? I heard you had some trouble with reporters," Kane said anxiously.

She swallowed a big hiccuping sigh. No need to upset him; she knew he'd had a hard day. "I'm f-fine."

"You don't sound fine."

Two fat tears dripped down her cheeks. "You don't know me well enough to know what's fine, and what isn't. How...how are the people who were hurt?"

"They're both in intensive care, but it looks hopeful."

"That's good news."

On the other end of the phone, Kane frowned. Beth didn't sound right, so maybe the reporters had upset her more than usual. He'd have to take steps to ensure it wouldn't happen again. People who messed with his family didn't like the consequences.

"Please tell me what's wrong," he prompted when she didn't say anything else.

Something that sounded suspiciously like a sniff came across the line and he shot out of his chair.

"*Beth*, what's wrong?"

"Razzle somehow got out. I can't find him anywhere."

"I'll be there as soon as possible."

"No. You're tired and there's nothing you can do." She sounded so dispirited it was like broken glass cutting his insides.

"Hang on, honey. I'm coming."

Kane immediately dialed the O'Rourke Industries helipad. The helicopter would get him to Crockett faster than driving. And while he was waiting for the bird to warm up, he started making other calls. He'd move heaven and earth if that's what it took to get Beth's kitten back.

There wasn't an answer when Kane knocked on Beth's door, so he went around and found her on the back steps. He sat next to her, searching for the right words.

"You're here," she whispered, her face wan in the evening light. She looked surprised, as if she hadn't really expected him. "You shouldn't have come, you've had a long day."

"It doesn't matter." Without waiting for permission

he plucked her into his lap and settled her against his chest. "We'll find him, honey. Don't worry."

She let out a shuddering sigh and her arms crept around his neck. "He's so curious. He must have gotten out when the photographer broke into the kitchen."

Kane got very still. "A photographer broke in?"

"I called the police. That took care of it."

He was furious. It was one thing to follow him and take pictures, quite another to invade Beth's privacy. He added the offense to the list of things he would be discussing with his security chief. "It won't happen again," he said with quiet certainty. "I promise."

"Do you think Razzle can find his way back to the house? He hasn't lived here for long, maybe he won't remember."

"I'm sure he will."

"It's just that he's so little."

Kane eased his hand under Beth's thick hair and rubbed the back of her neck. Damn it all, if he'd never involved her in his brother's scheme, she wouldn't have lost her kitten.

But whether Beth realized it or not, it wasn't just Razzle's disappearance upsetting her. She'd taken a risk on loving something else. She'd invited the two felines into her heart and now she might lose one of them.

The way she'd lost her fiancé.

Damn. Damn. *Damn.*

Sometimes life was hellishly unfair.

Beth slowly pried her eyes open and realized she was in her bed. Morning sun crept around the blinds someone had closed, and she was still wearing her shorts and T-shirt. Smoke was curled up against her back, giving himself a bath.

She'd barely started to think about the previous evening, when the door opened behind her.

"I know you don't like waking up early, but I thought you wouldn't mind a visitor," Kane said.

A loud *"merrooow"* screeched in her ear and his hand descended into her field of vision, holding an indignant kitten.

"Razzle."

Tears flooded her eyes as she clutched the kitten. Smoke scrambled out of the way as Beth turned over and looked at Kane.

"You found him."

He smiled. "I told you we'd get him back."

"Where was he?"

A trace of hardness crept into Kane's eyes. "I had my people track down the reporters who were at the house yesterday. Apparently Razzle decided to explore one of TV news' vans and the driver didn't realize it right away."

"But it's been hours and *hours* since Razzle disappeared. Why didn't he bring him back?"

"I think he was nervous about it," Kane said dryly. "And now he has the fear of God in him, so he's considering a move out of state. I wanted to suggest a different country, but my security chief was a wee bit softer on the issue."

Beth couldn't keep from smiling. Kane had mobilized the neighborhood to look for her baby, and apparently he'd called out his version of the National Guard after putting her to bed. But more than anything else, he'd comforted her when there had to be a million things more important to him.

"You're a wonderful man, Kane O'Rourke."

Kane played with a lock of her hair. "What brought that on? Not that I'm objecting, you understand. I like being called wonderful."

"You found my cat, for one thing. And you came back to be with me, when most men would have thought I was being silly to get so emotional."

He shook his head. "You weren't being silly. Anyway, my people found Razzle, and it was my fault there was a photographer snooping around your house."

"It was absolutely *not* your fault. Besides, you didn't know about the photographer when you came rushing back to Crockett."

"I was worried about you."

She covered his hand with her own. "It's been a long time since someone did something like that for me."

Kane didn't say anything for a moment, then he leaned down and kissed her forehead. "Honey, I think there are a lot of people who'd like to be there for you. I've never met someone with such a kind heart."

Beth closed her eyes, unwilling to let him see the thoughts and questions that might be revealed. It was hard being alone, but it was harder to love someone, then lose them. Wasn't it? How much risk did a person have to take? How many times could you pick up the pieces and still have the strength to keep going?

She wasn't even aware she'd asked the last question aloud until she heard Kane's long sigh. "I don't know, sweetheart, I've wondered that myself."

Her eyes popped open and she stared into his solemn face. "You have?"

"Each time I take my mother to the cemetery, or I remember how my youngest sister's husband ran off with her best friend, leaving her with two babies to raise alone. It makes you want to hide from pain, but things are going to happen, regardless. If you don't grab some of the good stuff, then you don't have anything when things go bad.''

"You have your family."

"I'm a lucky man. Which is fortunate for me, because I don't have your basic goodness, Beth. You could teach angels how to fly.''

She wanted to laugh and cry at the same time. Nobody had ever likened her to an angel. "That isn't true, I have a terrible temper.''

"And you're stubborn, too," Kane said. "But that's okay, because otherwise I'd be convinced I was about to buy the big one, and you were sent to see if I deserved a place in heaven.''

"You do.''

He surprised her by dropping a hard kiss on her mouth.

"What was that for?''

His hand caressed her jaw. "For looking at me that way. You have no idea how nice it makes me feel.''

"Oh." Beth set her kitten in a nest of blankets and Razzle curled up, tuckered out from his travels. "I'm going to fix us some breakfast," she said.

Things were getting more intense than either of them could handle. She needed the breathing space, even if he didn't.

Kane sat on the bed, letting the tension ease from his body. He still didn't know what he wanted from Beth, or what to do about her.

Friendship? Definitely. She was fun and smart and gave him a sense of peace he hadn't known in longer than he could remember. An intimate relationship? His response to Beth was hotter than an oil refinery fire. His conscience was telling him *no,* his body was screaming for the sweet oblivion he'd find in her arms. As for love, he was halfway there already. He didn't know how she felt, but love from a woman like Beth was worth more than all the money in the world.

Marriage was the big question. He'd thought he didn't have time for a wife, that it wouldn't be fair to Beth. But the past few days had changed the way he looked at things. And maybe the age difference wasn't such a problem. If two people were happy, did it really matter if one was eleven years older?

Razzle's sail-like ears stuck up from the rumpled ball he'd curled into, and Kane absently rubbed behind them. He'd been so determined to take care of his family after his father's death. The time he'd spent with Beth had made him realize he'd made it so important because he couldn't do anything to bring back his father.

A young man's picture smiled from a frame on the bedside table, and Kane lifted it, staring curiously. It had to be the hero. Beth's fiancé.

He loved danger.

I never knew when he'd risk everything....

"What the hell were you doing?" Kane muttered at the photo. "She was made for love and you damn well blew it. Now she's got her heart locked up tighter than Fort Knox."

The boyish smile didn't change, and Kane sighed. He couldn't fix the broken part of Beth's life, much as he wanted to. Certain things were beyond his ability, no matter how terrific it felt when she looked at him with those big eyes and told him he was wonderful.

He could only hope she'd open her heart and let him

in. Because it was the only place he wanted to go these days.

The next day traffic was heavy around the ballpark, but Kane navigated through it with his usual skill. Beth grinned wryly as she watched.

Kane did everything well.

The only reason he wasn't obnoxious was his complete lack of awareness that he *did* do everything well. There wasn't a self-indulgent bone in his body. He certainly wasn't what she'd expected a billionaire to be like. Hard work was second nature to Kane, and the money only seemed to matter because of the security it gave his family.

"Did you listen to your brother's radio station this morning?" she asked after they'd parked and were walking toward the northwest entrance of the stadium. "They've added the Wedding March as an intro to 'The O'Rourke Marriage Watch.'"

Kane grimaced. "I heard it. I told Pat he's getting carried away and to tone it down."

"Well, it's creative."

"That's not what I call it."

She laughed and shook her head. They were anonymous amongst hundreds of people streaming into the park, something she appreciated after the notoriety of their so-called romance. Even a billionaire couldn't compete with the excitement of baseball.

Kane stopped at one of the food stands. "Let's get some garlic fries," he suggested.

"No way."

He grinned over his shoulder. "Why? 'Fraid you'll have to kiss me later? It won't matter if we both eat them."

"Very funny." Beth gave his arm a shove. "We're having dinner with your family later. I don't want to be oozing garlic when I meet them."

"All right. But you're a real spoilsport." Kane put his arm around her waist and squeezed. "Fortunately you have some other nice features."

"Huh." She put a fair amount of disgust into the single word, but she was secretly pleased.

At the moment she felt pretty and happy. They were almost like any other couple at the park. Kane wore shorts that showed off the muscular strength of his legs, a suspiciously new-looking Mariners' shirt and a baseball cap. Between the cap and his sunglasses, he was practically unrecognizable. Normally she would have worn shorts as well, but since they were eating dinner with his family she'd opted for slacks and a light sweater top.

And her baseball glove, of course.

Even in the upper deck of the stadium you never knew when a fly ball might go in your direction.

But they didn't head for the upper level, instead Kane directed her to the lower deck in an area between the Mariners' dugout and home plate. "I thought you were getting seats higher up," she said, frowning slightly.

"These were the only ones available," Kane lied blandly. He gave Beth his most innocent look and nudged her down the narrow row. Libby had connections and she'd gotten her hands on a pair of prime season tickets for him.

"You shouldn't have done that," Beth scolded, not believing him for a minute.

"Shouldn't have done what?"

She shook her head and sank into her seat.

He hid a smile and sat next to her. Beth might object to his extravagance, but he could tell she was excited being so close to "her" baseball team. It wasn't surprising, she threw herself into everything with unqualified enthusiasm. At odd times he caught himself wondering how that enthusiasm would translate into the bedroom…and was pretty sure he already had the answer. If Beth let herself love, she'd love with a heart and passion that couldn't be measured.

"Have you ever been to a game?" she asked after a moment.

"We come once a year."

Each June Kane bought a block of tickets for his version of the "company picnic." He attended with his employees and their families, but was usually too busy making sure things went well to watch the game.

Today he'd be too busy watching Beth.

They sang the National Anthem and waited as the first pitch got thrown out. The Mariners' started out with a bang, nailing down six runs at the bottom of the first inning. Beth jumped to her feet, screaming and cheering along with everyone else.

There was only one bad moment when a ball came sailing right at her head. He reached out to deflect it, but she expertly caught the fly ball…right before handing it to a big-eyed child sitting in the row behind them.

About then Kane noticed the cameras were focused on them, so he hunched down and pulled his cap down over his forehead. To his relief, attention quickly shifted back to the action on the field.

Though he'd been too busy over the years to pay much attention to baseball, he found himself caught up in the game. Maybe it was Beth's influence, but he ended on his feet, cheering as the Mariners won with a score of eight to one.

Beth was so excited she threw her arms around his neck and gave him a happy kiss.

Before she could pull away, Kane put his hands at her waist. "Now that's what I call incentive for winning," he murmured.

"You weren't playing."

"No, I'm not playing," he said huskily.

The color in her gold-brown eyes darkened. Departing spectators jostled them closer and her breath quickened. "We...we should go."

But she didn't move and a contented sigh rose from Kane's chest. It would kill him to admit that his brother's "date with a billionaire" idea had turned out so well, yet it had. A tight feeling in his gut had relaxed, a feeling he hadn't even recognized because it was with him so long. He was like a badger who had dug underground for so long he'd forgotten what light was all about.

"Hey, Miss Cox," yelled a voice.

They both started and for an instant Kane was annoyed, thinking a reporter had found them, but it was one of the bat boys from the field.

"Yes?" she said.

"A little present from the team," the boy called, tossing her a baseball.

Beth snagged it out of the air, her mouth opening in an O of astonishment. As far as she could tell it was signed by all the players, the signatures crowding each other on the clean new surface of the ball.

"You arranged this," she said to Kane, unable to contain her pleased grin.

He shrugged. "It's no big deal. My assistant made

a couple of calls—it turns out she knows one of the team wives.''

If Kane had tried, he couldn't have gotten a present that pleased her more. Beth dropped the signed ball into her knapsack and kissed him again.

''Thank you,'' she said simply.

The crowd had thinned considerably by the time they reached his Mercedes, though they still had to wait while the lines of cars emptied from the parking garage.

It gave Beth time to get nervous again about meeting Kane's family. He'd made it clear they knew there wasn't a romance in the air, but she was torn between hoping to make a good impression, and worrying they wouldn't think she belonged. She had too much experience at not belonging.

Unable to sit still, she flipped the car visor down and shrieked. ''Why didn't you tell me my hair was such a mess?''

''Because it isn't.''

The car slid forward a few feet as she shook her head. ''You must be blind.'' She cast a sideways glance at him and glared. ''Don't you dare smile.''

''Was I?''

''Yes, and I want to know why.''

''Because I've never heard you fuss about your hair. You have beautiful hair, Beth. It looks great all tumbled down like that.''

''It looks like I just crawled out of bed,'' she grumbled.

''Yeah.''

The satisfied tone of Kane's voice made her flush. She was so confused. What did he want from her? Each time she convinced herself it was publicity and his desire to take care of his family, he made a comment that seemed...intimate. The thought distracted her so much she didn't think about meeting his mother until they were pulling into the driveway of a house that had been built around the same time as her own.

"Is that her house?" Beth asked, surprised. She'd expected something modern and high-tech, not this cozy place with the wide wraparound porch.

"Yes. She won't let me get something bigger—says it's too big already unless I give her some grandchildren to come visit." Kane sounded so disgruntled it almost took her mind off the upcoming introductions.

"You mentioned she wants more grandchildren."

"Mom loves kids."

He helped her out of the car and Beth brushed a small piece of lint from her green slacks. The windows of the old house were open and the sound of laughter rang in the air.

"Uh, is everyone here?"

She tugged nervously at the hem of her sweater top and tried to quell the butterflies in her tummy. It wasn't as if Kane was bringing her to "meet the family" in the traditional sense of the word. She couldn't deny they were becoming friends—annoying as he could be at times—and friends were invited to dinner without any expectations.

"Yup, I'm sure they're all here," Kane said comfortably. "There's no reason to be uneasy. They just want to meet the woman with the moxie to keep telling me 'no.'"

"Oh, that makes me feel better."

He grinned and tucked her arm into his elbow. "I guarantee they'll love you."

They walked inside, the laughter and voices enveloping them, along with the scent of pot roast. As Beth had feared, the entire O'Rourke clan had the same stunning good looks and easy sophistication as Kane and Shannon. She felt overwhelmed, even when his mother drew her out to the kitchen and hugged her.

"Mrs. O'Rourke?"

"Darling girl," the older woman said, smiling warmly. "I haven't seen my son so happy since we lost his father."

Instant panic clawed at Beth. "But we're not...it isn't like that. Kane said you knew we weren't involved."

"I know all about that nonsense." Peggy O'Rourke chuckled. She was a diminutive woman, with Kane's blue eyes and dark hair barely touched by gray. "I also know my son. You've given him something back, child. I don't care if he doesn't have the good sense to marry you, from now on you're a member of this family."

Quick tears burned in Beth's eyes. "That's nice of you."

"Nice nothing. I know quality when I see it. Now, I'm Mom to you, like everyone else. Isn't that right, Kane?"

Beth turned in time to see him standing in the doorway, an enigmatic expression on his face. She couldn't tell if he'd heard everything his mother had said, or just some of it.

"That's right," he agreed. "Shannon sent me out to see if you need help with dinner."

"Not Shannon's help," Peggy exclaimed with mock horror. "My eldest daughter is talented," she explained to Beth. "But she lacks a wee bit in domestic skills."

"That's like saying the Rock of Gibraltar is a pebble,'' Kane said dryly. ''If Shannon even *looks* at a kitchen, the fire alarm goes off.''

''I heard that,'' Shannon said, slapping him upside the head. ''You have no respect.''

''That's callin' the kettle black.''

He grinned easily and they continued to bicker, with various other siblings drifting in, joining the argument, then drifting out as they collected bowls and plates of food for the table. They seemed like any other family except for their amazing good looks.

Patrick O'Rourke arrived at the last moment, gave his mother a kiss, then grinned at Beth. He looked so much like Kane it startled her.

''Hey, nice to meet you, Beth Cox. You've been good for my business,'' he said.

''The 'O'Rourke Marriage Watch' has been good for your business,'' she retorted. ''I'm a helpless pawn in your publicity scheme.''

''Hardly helpless,'' Kane protested, holding a chair out for her. ''You've got me turning handstands.''

Chuckles greeted the remark, but nobody seemed to take it seriously. This was just the sort of big, noisy family Beth had always dreamed about. Still, it was hard to know how to act. They were so comfortable with one another, and she'd never had a family of any kind.

There was a quiet moment when they all took hands and bowed their heads. With Kane holding her fingers on one side, and Patrick O'Rourke on the other, Beth breathed her own silent prayer. Only it wasn't one of thankfulness, it was a plea for survival. She didn't want to love again, yet Kane was making serious inroads on her heart and self-sufficiency.

Dangerous inroads.

Apparently prayer was the only silent time the O'Rourkes observed. At any one time there were three or four conversations going on around the big table, but the subject they enjoyed the most was teasing Kane about his shaky single status.

"You have to be the first son to get married," said Shannon as she nibbled on a carrot. "It's tradition."

"Well, it's not going to be me," Patrick declared. "I'm a bachelor for life, though I think Beth will be a great sister-in-law." He winked at Beth, who wanted to crawl beneath the table.

"Don't tease her," Peggy scolded.

Under cover of the tablecloth Kane squeezed Beth's knee. "This is their idea of being nice," he whispered. "Don't mind anything they say."

She did mind, but not in the way he thought. It didn't matter how warmly they welcomed her, she didn't belong. The jokes about her marrying Kane only emphasized that.

Married?

They obviously didn't understand. Kane would never consider her as a wife.

A wistful pang went through her. But what if he did, by some miracle, decide he wanted marriage? He seemed to like her, and kissing him was like spontaneous combustion.

Maybe she was really worried about losing everything. Maybe she'd discovered that comfortable wasn't safe, it was just dull—and the real problem was that she didn't believe Kane could ever love her, so it was easier to believe it couldn't happen.

"By the way, Beth, I really appreciate the chance to run an empire," Neil O'Rourke said, catching her attention. "If it wasn't for your distracting influence on Kane, I wouldn't be getting the chance."

He was obviously joking, but it was equally obvious how much he thought of his brother. They all did. Kane had taken the place of their father, no matter how much they chafed against his protectiveness.

"Just don't lose my shirt," Kane warned. "A few million is all right, but let's keep the damage minimal."

"You're a richer man today because of me," Neil responded, grinning. "By more than a few million. Keep him out of my way, Beth, and I'll double his money in a month."

It was all lighthearted, but the idea of losing or gaining millions of dollars was more than she could comfortably handle. "I'll get some more water," she said, grabbing the empty pitcher.

"Let Patrick get it, he's closest," Shannon protested, but Beth shook her head.

A worried frown creased Kane's forehead as Beth disappeared into the kitchen. He knew she wasn't comfortable with his family. If only he could reassure her. She was so special, she made the rest of his life seem trivial by comparison.

He got up and his brothers and sisters got quiet, suddenly realizing they might have gone too far with their lighthearted teasing.

"We didn't mean anything," Shannon said. "Did we upset her?"

"I don't know, I'm going to find out."

He found Beth at the back door, gazing out at the field behind the house. Kane gathered her close and inhaled the sweet scent of her hair.

"They get to me sometimes, too," he murmured. "Never a quiet moment with the O'Rourkes."

"I shouldn't have come."

God. She was the most precious woman in the world, but this was hardly the place to talk privately. Any minute his family would all come pouring out, wanting to apologize and sweep her back with them again.

"Of course you had to come," he said firmly. "You didn't want me to face them alone, did you?"

"They adore you."

"They drive me crazy. The only time I get any peace and quiet is when they're asleep. I love coming to your house—it's actually sane there."

Her soft laugh rewarded him. "Sane? Right. Bursting water pipes, painting, hysterical kittens—sounds perfectly normal."

"Perfectly wonderful," Kane corrected.

She had no idea how wonderful.

Someone cleared their throat behind them, and he looked over his shoulder to see nine pairs of worried eyes staring at him. He scowled, wishing they would go away.

"Beth, darlin'," said his mother, her brogue deepening. "I know we take some gettin' used to, but don't give up on us."

Beth drew a deep breath. It seemed easier to face them again with Kane's arms around her, though it should have been embarrassing. She wasn't his girlfriend. She wasn't even his lover, and they all knew it.

The teasing was just that, teasing.

She plastered a smile on her face. "It's all right. You're nothing compared to a hoard of newspaper reporters wanting to know why I turned down a date with a billionaire.''

They chuckled and seemed relieved, but it was Kane's tender look that turned her inside out.

Chapter Ten

"**I** think this is the last one," Peggy said, handing Beth a pot to dry. The dishes had gone into the state-of-the-art dishwasher.

Peggy had protested Beth's offer to help with the dishes, but she'd insisted. If nothing else, it gave her something to do with her hands so she didn't feel so out of place.

Kane and his brothers were taking expansion leaves from the dining-room table and storing them in a hidden closet, arguing all the while about some European soccer team. Beth didn't know anything about soccer and she'd never been to Europe, but it was fascinating to listen to the good-natured sparring. There had never been happy arguments in her foster home, only bitter rancor and coldness.

"Oh, please. Change the subject. Sports are boring," Kathleen O'Rourke said as she wiped the oak table with furniture polish. She was the youngest of the siblings and the mother of three-year-old twin girls.

"Chicks never like sports," Neil said, only to get slapped in the face with a polish-laden dust rag.

"Hey, Beth is a Mariners' fan," Kane said, pulling her down on the couch with him. "She listens to games on the radio, and everything."

His brothers groaned and said it wasn't fair, none of *their* girlfriends had ever liked baseball, and how did Kane get so lucky? At the last minute they caught themselves and shuffled their feet in discomfort.

Beth suspected they had been warned to be careful what they said, but it wasn't their fault she didn't belong. They were trying their best to make her welcome, they just naturally wanted to tease their big brother. The amazing thing was how well he took it.

"I understand KLMS has picked up a lot of new listeners," she said in an attempt to lighten the mood. "So the contest promotion worked."

"We've more than doubled our market base," Patrick enthused. "You've been a good sport to go along with everything. I'm sure sorry about what happened with those reporters. At least the kitten turned up all right."

Kane was holding her hand and she squeezed it tighter. "Your brother took care of it. He was wonderful."

"Not so wonderful on my end. He called and blistered my ears so bad it's a miracle I still have my hearing," Patrick griped, but it was without heat. The affection between the two men was obvious. They might not have settled the inevitable issues that arose between brothers, yet it didn't make any fundamental difference to their relationship.

"We could have avoided the whole thing if he would just let me invest in the station," Kane growled.

"No way."

"I don't see anything wrong with a silent investor."

"Really," Beth chided. "Could you be silent about anything, Kane? Patrick wants to make it on his own like you did. Let him prove he can do it."

"I'm sure he can do it, but why not make it easier?"

"Because easier isn't always best," she said gently. "And it doesn't nearly mean as much. You know that. Nothing worth having is easy."

Kane's eyes widened as he remembered his father saying exactly the same thing. *Nothing worth having is easy, son. You've got to earn your place in the world so you can stand up as a man.*

Damn.

He looked around at the grinning faces of his brothers and sisters. They were delighted with Beth's championship of Patrick's independence—and by extension, their own. Okay, so maybe he was having trouble letting go. And he might have been interfering in their lives, rather than standing back and letting them come for help if they needed it.

But it was hard.

He missed the 2:00 a.m. calls for help and advice and an ear to listen to, though he'd griped plenty at the time. Now they'd all gone on to their own lives and he wanted to be needed the way he used to be.

He gazed down at Beth's face and breathed a prayer of thankfulness that he'd found her before it was too late. Of course, that also meant he'd have to acknowledge to Patrick that things had turned out all right.

At least...he hoped it would be all right.

There were no guarantees when it came to broken hearts and new dreams. What he really needed to do was get her out of this house and kiss her into silence.

He was thinking a lot about kissing Beth these days, and about holding her close every night for a lifetime.

"We'd better head back to Crockett," he suggested after another few minutes. "The ferry doesn't run as often in the evening."

"I wish you'd let me come over in my own car," Beth said, distressed all over again. "It's too much to drive back and forth twice in one day." They'd argued about it several times, but she'd finally given in and let him pick her up in Crockett—stubbornness went two ways.

"You're welcome to stay with me," Peggy offered. "I love to have company."

"Beth probably wants to get home to the children," Kane said easily. "You know how it is with new cat mothers."

At Beth's request he went out to the Mercedes to get the homegrown vegetables she'd brought for his mother, having forgotten them when they first arrived.

When he carried the heavily laden box into the kitchen, his mother caught his arm. "Are you going to propose to that dear child, or not?"

Pegeen O'Rourke had never been shy about stating an opinion, and apparently her opinion was that Beth Cox should become her daughter-in-law.

Kane sighed. "It isn't that easy."

"Open your mouth and say 'I love you, Beth.' Then ask her to be your wife. That seems quite easy."

A ghost of a smile creased his mouth. "Pegeen O'Rourke, did my father propose to you, or was it the other way around?"

His mother just laughed.

"I'm still deciding what to do," Kane continued

more seriously. "She's been hurt so badly. Maybe it's too soon to say anything."

"You'll never know if you don't ask."

"She might say no. She's good at that, remember?"

"Hmm. I see your point."

Kane rubbed the back of his neck. "Tell me something, Mom. About Dad...do you ever hear him as if he's talking to you now, not simply like something you remember?"

His mom put her hand under his chin and looked into his eyes, just the way she did when he was little and wanted him to especially pay attention. "I hear him all the time, son, talking to my heart. It helps get me through, and I pray each night my children will find the same kind of love. You do love Beth, don't you? I'm not wrong about that."

"No. You aren't wrong." Emotion clogged his throat and he cleared it impatiently.

He'd fought his feelings long and hard, but he loved Beth so much it was all he could think about. She had a unique beauty that went beyond her face and figure, though both were just fine in his eyes. And her soul...she was so sweet and decent it made him cling to the moments they were together, and hold them in his heart to keep him warm when they weren't.

When he'd gained control of his emotions he went out to the living room, kissed his sisters and nieces goodbye, and then his mother. "Don't worry, I'll think of something," he whispered in her ear.

Peggy gave him a confident smile. "I know, lad. You're like your father. He didn't know how to fail, either."

They were on the road, wrapped in the velvet darkness of the Mercedes, when Kane heard Beth let out a pent-up breath. "I'm sorry I interfered," she said. "Back when you were talking to Patrick. It wasn't my business to say anything."

He shook his head, though she couldn't see it in the dark. "You didn't interfere. I may not have liked it, but you had every right to say the things you did."

She was silent for a long minute. "Kane, part of filling your father's shoes is knowing when to let go."

"Yeah. It's a hell of a thing—if you do everything right, you obsolete yourself right out of a job." He slapped the steering wheel with the palm of his hand, unable to control his frustration. "It's just that I have all this money and I want to make their lives easier."

The soft leather of the passenger seat whispered as Beth slid closer and put her hand on his arm. Kane knew she hadn't done it to excite him sexually, but it was like a brand touching him.

"You have to stop believing money is the most important thing you give, because you're wrong," she said quietly. "I can see how much they look up to you. You're the solid foundation that lets them fly, because there's a safe place to return if it's needed."

"I wish you wouldn't say things like that," he said hoarsely. "Because it makes me want to kiss you senseless."

Though Beth had withdrawn her hand, he heard a sharp intake of her breath, and then a drawn-out sigh.

"We're on the freeway," she said.

"I could solve that problem fast enough."

"Maybe you'd better wait. Sleep on it for the night, then see how you feel."

It wasn't a complete rejection. In fact, it wasn't a rejection at all. Beth being Beth, just wanted him to be sure. And an idea popped into his head, the best way to propose to such a stubborn, terrific lady. But first he'd have to talk to Patrick and set everything up.

Then he'd propose, and pray that for once, she'd say yes.

"All right," Kane agreed. "We'll talk about it tomorrow. But I don't see me changing my mind."

Patrick stared incredulously over the pile of compact discs on his desk. "You want to what?"

"I want to propose to Beth on the radio."

"Don't you think that's risky? What if she says no?"

"Thanks for pointing out that unpleasant possibility. It never once occurred to me."

"Well, she does have a track record in that department, and you didn't like it much the first time," said his brother, obviously too rattled to recognize sarcasm when he heard it.

Kane thought about how far he'd come since the day he'd read that a certain Bethany Cox had refused her prize date with a billionaire. His pride had been wounded and he hadn't really stopped to think what led her to such a decision. Now he knew if she said "no" to marrying him, it wouldn't matter what the public thought. He'd never stop loving and needing her, nor would he stop trying to convince her they were meant for each other.

He looked his brother in the eye. "Patrick, Beth doesn't believe she's beautiful or glamorous enough for me...that *I* don't think she's beautiful or glamorous enough."

"Don't be ridiculous. She's hot."

Kane lifted an eyebrow. "Maybe you want to rephrase that since she's going to be your sister-in-law," he said sternly. Old habits were hard to break, and he'd done plenty of stern talking to Patrick over the years.

Patrick sighed. "I didn't mean she was hot to me, but I can appreciate her being a great-looking babe. Personally I think you're too ugly for her, but if she can stand it, then it's not my problem."

Kane laughed. "Look, she needs to know I'm willing to tell the world, take the chance of being turned down because she's worth that much to me," he explained. "So, how about it? If nothing else, your station deserves the news scoop since you're the reason we met."

A slow smile grew on his brother's face. "Sounds like good publicity to me."

It was almost eleven in the morning and Kane hadn't arrived, a fact that Beth was trying, without success, to ignore.

Her store was closed Sundays and Mondays, so she didn't have any excuse to leave. Her business partner still hadn't gone into labor with her second child, so she wasn't baby-sitting Emily's little girl. And she was generally going crazy.

"Why did I interfere?" she moaned, thumping her head on the table.

She should have kept her mouth shut and not said those things. Kane was a smart guy; he'd have figured out sooner or later that his family needed breathing room. He'd just been polite when he accepted her apology.

In the beginning she'd been desperate to chase him out of her life, maybe she'd succeeded.

"Be careful what you ask for," Beth muttered in a dire voice. Of course, it might have nothing to do with what she'd said. He might have realized she was too awkward and uncomfortable with his family to ever belong.

Like she ever had any of hope of belonging to begin with.

She did love them, though. She loved *him* more than anything, but the rest of the O'Rourkes were wonderful, too.

Beth slumped backward in her chair and stared at the sink that Kane had installed. The plumbing now worked like a dream. No more slow drains or leaky faucet, and each time she used it, she thought of him.

Maybe she'd have to move.

The phone rang, making her jump. She would have ignored it, but she couldn't because it might be either Kane or her very pregnant business partner.

"Hello."

"Is this Beth Cox?"

In the back of her mind she realized the voice sounded familiar, but she was too miserable to care.

"Yes."

"Great. This is KLMS calling, and we're transmitting to the greater Seattle area."

Beth put a death grip on the receiver of her phone. She wasn't in the mood for "The O'Rourke Marriage Watch." She never wanted to hear those ridiculous words again.

"I don't—"

"Hold on for just a moment," the man said cheerfully. "I have someone waiting to ask you a very important question."

In the van outside Beth's house, Kane swallowed the tension gripping him and took the transmitter set. The

DJ gave him a thumbs-up signal and they shared a mutual grin.

"Beth? This is Kane."

"Oh, hi."

Her voice was faint, so he couldn't tell if she was happy or angry, or anything in-between. Well, it didn't matter. He was proposing and wouldn't take no for an answer.

"Bethany Cox, I'm so crazy in love with you I can't sleep at night. Will you marry me?"

There was a gasp on the other end of the phone, followed by a dull thud.

"Honey, are you all right?" Kane demanded urgently.

There wasn't an answer, and without a thought he dove for the door of the van. The DJ's eyes widened and he barely had time to keep the transmitter set from being ripped out of the panel.

Kane found Beth on the kitchen floor. She was rubbing her bottom, looking dazed.

"What happened?" he asked as he knelt by her.

"I missed the chair," Beth whispered. "And the phone's broken." She jiggled the receiver and Kane's gaze followed the cord; it was no longer connected to the wall.

"That's all right, honey. We'll get it repaired."

He carefully helped her up and wrapped her in his arms. Damn, she felt good.

"I should have done it different," he whispered into her hair. "Champagne and flowers and candlelight—a traditional proposal on one knee. But I wanted something special, just like you."

Beth's head was still reeling. She could barely take it in that Kane had actually proposed. On the radio, no less! He couldn't know she'd say yes, but he'd taken the risk of publicly embarrassing himself, just to reassure her.

"I'm not special."

"Don't give me that, lady. You've had me tied into knots since the day we met," he growled. "And if I don't make love to you soon I'm going to be permanently disabled."

She sniffed, hiding the fact she was secretly thrilled. "That's just sex."

"Don't knock it," Kane said, giving her a little shake. "But I'm not talking about the kind of sex you can walk away from, I'm talking about the blow-your-head-off, died-and-think-I've-gone-to-heaven, can't-ever-give-it-up sort of loving."

"Oh. I guess that would be different."

"You bet it is."

Beth snuggled her cheek into the hollow between Kane's chest and left shoulder and felt the hard pounding of his heart. There was a lot left to be said, but she needed some of the adrenaline in her system to settle before she could think coherently.

Kane's fingers smoothed her hair, slid over her shoulders and back, then settled on her bottom in exactly the place she'd bumped it. He rubbed in slow circles that should have been soothing, but weren't in the least.

"Patrick says I'm too ugly for a hot babe like you," he said, just as if he wasn't making all that adrenaline get worse instead of better. "But that if you can stand it, it's not his problem."

"I'm not hot," she mumbled, still wanting reassurance.

"Wanna bet?"

His finger skimmed under the high hem of her shorts, finding ticklish skin, and she squirmed.

"Kane."

"Just making sure you're paying attention, honey."

"I'm paying attention."

You don't know how much.

Proposing on the radio was silly and romantic and *wonderful.* Maybe it didn't matter the way the world saw her, as long as Kane saw the woman he wanted.

Except…she also had to think about his family. They were an intrinsic part of Kane's life and she hadn't exactly made a good impression on them. But when she said as much, he looked at her as if she'd lost her mind.

"Bad impression? What the hell are you talking about? They're crazy about you."

"They were nice," she said, shaking her head. "But it's obvious I don't belong. You're high society, and I'm incredibly *not.*"

Kane made a noise that sounded suspiciously like a snort. "High society? Not a chance. We're ordinary people, Beth. Irish immigrants who arrived in this country with barely a dime to call our own. As for not belonging…" He kissed the inside of her wrist. "Mom is already looking at bridal magazines and planning the wedding. She thinks you're the sweetest thing imaginable and will disown me if we don't get married."

He grinned.

"Naturally she doesn't know about your stubborn streak yet. But I'm betting she'll think that's great, too."

"I'm not stubborn."

"Yeah, right. And I'm the Easter Bunny."

Kane's eyes were so full of love it took Beth's breath

away, and she realized the choice was already made. He'd stolen her heart so completely she'd never get it back. She could marry him, knowing bad things sometimes happened, or she could die a piece at a time, each day worse than the last because they weren't together.

Of course, she shouldn't let him off the hook so easily, and she knew exactly what to say—something guaranteed to get some fireworks going.

"The truth is, you just want to marry me to help your brother," she mused. "A wedding would get even more publicity than a date."

"That's a damned idiotic thing to say," Kane roared, instantly outraged. "How could you even *think* such a thing?"

"You've spent your entire adult life taking care of your brothers and sisters," she said reasonably.

"They can just take care of themselves from now on. The only person I plan to take care of is you, even if you are the most stubborn, unreasonable, *impossible* woman I've ever known," he snapped.

"How about babies?"

The question threw him. "Babies?"

"I assume we'll want to have some babies. But only one to begin with, if that's all right. Don't you want to take care of them as well? And by the way, it isn't politically correct to tell a woman you want to take care of her."

It was then that Kane spied the smile tugging at Beth's lips. A chuckle rolled out of his chest, growing until it was a full-throated laugh. "What can I say? I'm a throwback to caveman days. It's genetic."

She patted his cheek and gave him a breathtaking smile. "How about just saying we'll take care of each other?"

He couldn't imagine anything better, because Beth was a woman who could do it all—partner, wife, mother of his children...lover. He was particularly looking forward to the lover part.

"That's perfect," he murmured, framing her face in his hands. "But isn't there something you have to tell me? Something important you might have forgotten?"

Her nose wrinkled in confusion, then her lips curved. "There certainly is. I love you, Kane O'Rourke. So much it frightens me. The best day of my life was when I won that silly contest."

He pulled her back against his heart, whispering his love and hearing it sweetly returned. Beth might have won the contest, but he was the one who got the real prize.

Epilogue

"Close your eyes, sweetheart."

"But I can't see that way."

Kane chuckled. "I know. That's the whole point."

Shifting his bride in his arms, he managed to punch the elevator button. The door closed with a silent whoosh, and the car rose smoothly.

"Don't tell me, we're having a picnic for our wedding dinner," Beth said. "Ants, hot dogs and everything." Still keeping her eyes closed, she nuzzled his neck, touching the tip of her tongue to his carotid artery.

Kane groaned and nearly dropped her.

They'd gotten married relatively quickly—just four weeks after his proposal—but it had seemed like forever. Apparently even the simplest wedding required endless fittings, meetings with bridal consultants and hours of poring over every imaginable book and magazine on the subject.

And that was just his mother; his sisters had been worse.

Beth just smiled serenely through the whole thing, her nerves only showing when they were alone together—which in Kane's opinion hadn't happened nearly enough.

But the wait was finally over.

He had his wife to himself; just the two of them, a huge bed, and no family. Luckily he had the resources to ensure their privacy. Beth would squawk when she discovered he'd booked the entire floor for their honeymoon, but teasing her out of a snit was too much fun for him to mind.

"We're not having a picnic," he said. "How does Dom Pérignon and strawberries sound to start?"

She made a huffy sound. "Expensive."

Kane chuckled. He didn't think Beth would ever be comfortable being the wife of a billionaire, but he enjoyed reminding her of all the good she could do with their money.

"Have I mentioned how beautiful you are, Mrs. O'Rourke?"

"Not in the last five minutes. Can I open my eyes now?"

"You'll have to wait a little longer."

The elevator opened and he carried her toward the last flight of steps, nodding at the security men he had posted as an extra guarantee they wouldn't be disturbed. They were consummate professionals and never even cracked a smile at the sight of their boss acting like any other besotted bridegroom.

"Where are we going, outer Mongolia?" Beth asked as she swayed against him during the climb.

"Nope." He walked into their room, one of the Victorian "attic" suites offered by the hotel. "You can look now."

Beth opened her eyes and let out a delighted cry. "It's wonderful," she said.

"It seemed appropriate—this is where we were originally supposed to stay on our first date. Separate rooms, of course." Kane kissed her gently, reluctant to put her down because it felt so nice holding his wife that way.

His wife.

Two words that had the power to bring him to his knees.

When he finally laid Beth on the four-poster bed, his breath was coming fast. She was so lovely, her face glowing with the kind of happiness he knew was reflected in his own eyes.

He cleared his throat. It wouldn't be sensitive of him to suggest they rip off their wedding finery and fall into bed, so he backed off and tried to be patient.

"I…I'll let in some air."

Beth watched Kane cross to the window and swing it open. He stood for a while, breathing the night air and gazing out at the harbor. She could hardly believe he belonged to her, or the way her life had changed in the past month. It was as if they had been created for each other, in the special way that lucky men and women had felt since the world began.

There were still times she felt uncomfortable with his family, but the O'Rourkes were the determined type, cutting right through the awkward moments with hugs and laughter. The only thing that seemed to matter to them was that she made Kane happy.

Shaking out the heavy skirt of her wedding dress, Beth looked around. They were at the very top of the hotel, in one of the Victorian suites Emily had extolled as being the "most romantic place you can imagine."

Dozens of creamy-white roses filled the air with a gentle fragrance, though a single flame-red rose lay on the table where a champagne bucket and strawberries also waited.

Beth picked it up, a secret smile filling her.

Maybe it wasn't the room that was romantic, but the man she'd married.

She poured the champagne and brought a glass to Kane, leaving the strawberries. Truthfully she wasn't hungry. They had eaten a little at the reception, and too many butterflies were dancing in her tummy to consider anything else.

"We could have had a bigger wedding if you'd wanted it," he said, slanting a kiss across her lips. "We didn't have to come back to Victoria."

Beth shook her head. "I wanted it this way, too. It was perfect."

They managed to keep the press from bothering them by agreeing to pictures after the ceremony, so the wedding had stayed the intimate affair they had both hoped for—just Kane's family and a few friends, including Emily and Nick with their daughter and new baby son.

Everyone else was partying in one of the hotel's private banquet rooms, but Kane had finally suggested they slip away to their own "celebration." Anticipation had grown with each glance and touch they'd shared; now Beth wondered if she'd hyperventilate before they made it into bed.

"By the way," he murmured, "you still haven't answered my question."

Beth frowned, trying to think what he was talking about. "What question?"

"You never said yes, you'd marry me. Honestly, I've never known a more contrary woman," Kane said with mock exasperation."

She managed a smile.

The spacious room seemed to shrink as he leaned over her, kissing her with a gentle patience that seemed at odds with the teasing heat in his eyes. She couldn't help remembering that he had lots of experience, while she was a neophyte with only a few spicy kisses to guide her.

"I'm glad we waited," he said simply, referring to their decision to wait before making love. Old dreams and ideas were hard to let go, and now she'd have the traditional wedding night she'd once planned to share with another man.

One of the things they had done during the past month was really talk about Curt. Beth didn't want any ghosts in their marriage, even ghosts that Kane only feared were there. Curtis Martin had been a good man, but he wasn't Kane O'Rourke. Kane had shown her a world of love beyond anything she'd ever dreamed.

Her heart belonged to him, wholly and completely.

"Um...I think I'll change," she said, and saw a fierce satisfaction in Kane's face.

Before she could change her mind, Beth scooped up the nightgown draped across a pillow and hurried into the bathroom. She no longer worried that Kane wouldn't be satisfied with her body, but she had nervous jitters dancing in her tummy. Making love was something of a mystery. Oh, she knew what went where, but knowing and actually understanding it were two different things.

Her wedding dress was made of antique lace and crystal beads over a crepe silk underskirt. Simple and elegant, it must have cost a fortune, though her mother-in-law-to-be had pooh-poohed the cost. Beth carefully put it on a hanger and donned the nightgown that Shannon had given her at a bridal shower. The gown clung to her curves, leaving nothing to the imagination. It practically screamed, "Come and get me, I'm not wearing anything underneath."

At least, that's what Shannon had claimed it said. Her knowing wink hadn't shown any mercy for Beth's warm face.

Well, they'd promised to love each for better or for worse. And her husband would just have to be patient while she was figuring out what he liked the best.

She swallowed and opened the door.

Kane looked at Beth in her white satin gown and groaned. The soft light turned her skin golden and she seemed too delicate and otherworldly to be real. Then he remembered the wedding toast she'd surprised him with at the reception, and his heart expanded with pride.

To my remarkable husband. I've never known a man more deserving to be called a hero. I'll love you forever, and even that won't be long enough.

"More champagne?" he asked, his voice almost unrecognizable.

Beth shook her head. She was breathing quickly, and like a magnet, his attention was drawn to the rise and fall of her breasts.

"I'll get my wedding dress out of the way so you can use the bathroom," she said.

"Wait." Kane's arm shot out, blocking the door.

"The thing is," he said quietly. "I'm a little nervous here. I love you to the bottom of my soul, and I need you so badly I can't hardly think. How...um...how do you want to...start?"

An incredulous wonder filled Beth.

He meant it. Her dear, wonderful husband was nervous about making love to her.

"I think we could start here," she whispered, reaching up slowly to slip the spaghetti strap of her gown off her shoulder. She flipped the second one down her other arm, and wiggled slightly.

Kane felt as if he'd been hit with a forklift. The thin satin slid down, its progress only impeded by the thrust of her nipples. The fabric clung precariously, those sweet points hardening beneath his gaze. With a smile he leaned close and caught one of the straps with his teeth. It only took a little tugging and pulling to drop it in a heap on the carpet.

He stepped backward, his gaze sweeping Beth's body. She was a study in elegance, with small, perfectly shaped breasts and hips that flared gently from a slim waist.

"Kane?"

"I've dreamed about this," he muttered. "And now I'm going to have a heart attack. That's why old guys shouldn't marry sexy young things like you—it's too hard on their system."

Beth laughed. "You're only thirty-seven. That's not old."

"Oh, good. I may live after all."

Sweeping his hands beneath her, he lifted his wife again and laid her on the bed.

"Things have been so rushed," Beth whispered,

"and I didn't think to discuss it with you, but...I'm not on the pill."

If possible, his body grew ever harder. "I'm glad," Kane said with heavy satisfaction.

Beth moved restlessly, wondering at the grabbing sensation at the base of her stomach. Kane had barely touched her and yet she felt prickles of heat and electricity everywhere. She wanted him to go faster, so she rose on her knees.

"Do you mind?" she purred, unbuttoning the shirt he wore. "I've waited for twenty-six years to do this." Swaying forward, she kissed his jaw, brushing her nipples over the wedge of chest hair she'd uncovered.

Kane moved so quickly it took her breath away. One minute she was kneeling in front of him, the next they were both naked and in the bed.

His exploring fingers made her squirm and sigh, and she had an equal effect on him. The tingling in her abdomen grew so bad she couldn't keep from squirming, which seemed to be all right with Kane until she felt him nudging between her legs.

"Oh..." She jerked.

Catching her hips, he held her perfectly still.

"Easy," he soothed. "Slow and easy this time."

He gave her time to adjust as he pressed downward, wincing visibly as she absorbed the slight flash of discomfort. And then they were so deeply joined she couldn't believe they'd ever been apart. He seemed to know when the balance shifted, her muscles no longer tight from instinctively trying to reject him, but tensing for another reason, this one far more pleasant.

It only took another deep thrust to send her over the edge, and she fell, sensations exploding beyond anything she could have imagined.

Much later, Beth lay with her head on Kane's shoulder. It was a lot to absorb, the power of two people being together. And she felt a little embarrassed going off like a firecracker and leaving him behind.

"I'm sorry," she whispered.

"About what?" Kane asked, clearly astonished.

"About…not waiting."

He chuckled. "Don't go apologizing. A man likes to know he's appreciated. And besides…" His forefinger circled her nipple and she moaned. "You caught up again, real quick."

"Is it always going to be like that?"

Kane pulled her over him, delighting in the feel of her silken skin. "It's only going to get better."

"I don't know if that's possible."

He looked into Beth's eyes and saw the promise of forever shining in them. "Love makes everything possible. Now be quiet and kiss me."

She smiled, finally doing exactly what he asked.

*   *   *   *   *

If you enjoyed what you just read,
then we've got an offer you can't resist!

Take 2 bestselling love stories FREE!

Plus get a FREE surprise gift!

*Silhouette presents an exciting
new continuity series:*

**When a royal family rolls out the red carpet
for love, power and deception, will their
lives change forever?**

The saga begins in April 2002 with:

The Princess Is Pregnant!

by Laurie Paige (SE #1459)

**May: THE PRINCESS AND THE DUKE by Allison Leigh
(SE #1465)**

**June: ROYAL PROTOCOL by Christine Flynn
(SE #1471)**

Be sure to catch all nine Crown and Glory stories: the first three appear in
Silhouette Special Edition, the next three continue in Silhouette Romance
and the saga concludes with three books in Silhouette Desire.

And be sure not to miss more royal stories,
from Silhouette Intimate Moments'

Romancing
the Crown,

running January through December.

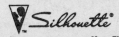

Start Your Summer With Sizzle
And Silhouette Books!

In June 2002, look for these HOT volumes led by *New York Times* bestselling authors and receive a free Gourmet Garden kit!

Retail value of $17.00 U.S.

THE BLUEST EYES IN TEXAS by Joan Johnston
and WIFE IN NAME ONLY by Carolyn Zane

THE LEOPARD'S WOMAN by Linda Lael Miller
and WHITE WOLF by Lindsay McKenna

THE BOUNTY by Rebecca Brandewyne
and A LITTLE TEXAS TWO-STEP by Peggy Moreland

OVERLOAD by Linda Howard
and IF A MAN ANSWERS by Merline Lovelace

This exciting promotion is available at your favorite retail outlet. See inside books for details.

Only from

Silhouette®
Where love comes alive™

Visit Silhouette at www.eHarlequin.com

PSNCP02